BREAKING THE RULES

Who broke into teacher Julia's car to steal Year Eleven's English coursework — and why? Attempting to solve the mystery, Julia soon finds herself *Breaking the Rules* . . . In *Running*, Mick Ashworth witnesses a murder. When he gives evidence in court, his family is put in jeopardy and they are forced to go into hiding under the witness protection scheme. Can they keep their new identities secret? And in *Beloved*, Helen begins a happy relationship with Stefan — but things soon start to take a sinister turn . . .

D1394465

Books by Geraldine Ryan
in the Linford Mystery Library:

LEAVE OVER
CURTAIN CALL
CASEY CLUNES INVESTIGATES
AN INSPECTOR CALLS
A STORM IN A TEACUP
SCHOOL FOR SCANDAL
MORTAL PROSE

GERALDINE RYAN

BREAKING THE RULES
and Other Stories

Complete and Unabridged

LINFORD
Leicester

First published in Great Britain

First Linford Edition
published 2014

Copyright © 2012 by Geraldine Ryan
All rights reserved

A catalogue record for this book is available
from the British Library.

ISBN 978–1–4448–2161–1

Published by
F. A. Thorpe (Publishing)
Anstey, Leicestershire

Set by Words & Graphics Ltd.
Anstey, Leicestershire
Printed and bound in Great Britain by
T. J. International Ltd., Padstow, Cornwall

This book is printed on acid-free paper

RENFREW DISTRICT
ARTS AND LIBRARIES
COUNCIL

1 885237 21

Contents

Breaking the Rules

1

It was already getting dark as Julia picked her way through the wasteland jokingly referred to as the school overflow car park.

She swore under her breath as she narrowly missed tripping over a loose stone that could easily have sent her — along with the thirty buff folders she was loaded up with — into a sprawling heap.

If she'd got out of bed when the alarm went off, instead of creeping further under the duvet, trying to kid herself it was Sunday and not Monday, she'd have easily managed to grab a spot in the main car park, a mere lurch away from the entrance to the school where she taught, and where there was not only Tarmac but lights and CCTV.

Had it not been for the cutbacks, there would have been funding available to set this bit of wasteland to rights. As it was, all renovations and repairs had been put on hold until such time as the economic situation improved. Julia wasn't holding her breath.

Up ahead, her little red car beckoned to her cheerfully, and her heart lifted briefly at the sight of it. Then she remembered what lay ahead this evening. All thirty of these English coursework files had to be in order for Wednesday's moderation meeting — a tedious and long-drawn-out affair in which she and her colleagues cross-marked one another's students' essays to make sure that they were all assessing to the same standard.

A movement up ahead stopped her in her tracks. Peering through the gloom, she thought she saw someone hanging around by her car. The trick was to walk with confidence. She reminded herself she was five foot eight and a curvaceous size 14 and more than capable of taking care of herself. As she got nearer, she almost fainted with relief when she realised that it was a very small boy.

'Miss?'

4

She peered down at the boy from over her folders. She didn't recognise him, but then Dooley Park contained over a thousand pupils. Contained being the operative word, Julia sometimes thought.

'Shouldn't you be at home by now, young man? It's gone five,' she said.

The boy looked up at her with innocent eyes.

'I was going home, Miss. But then I remembered I left my PE kit in the changing rooms.'

'So why didn't you go back and get it?'

'I only remembered when I was nearly home. I was at the park. I'm too scared to go in, in case I get into trouble with Sir.'

Julia sympathised. As a lifelong exercise shirker, her own experience of PE staff when she'd been at school had not been at all good. In fact, she'd always found them to be a breed apart.

'Where did you leave your bag? Can you remember?' she asked him.

He blinked. 'It was in the boys' changing room, just by the door,' he said, looking hopeful. He'd been there last lesson.

'Hang on while I put these in my car,' she said. 'Then I'll just nip back and get it for you. You might as well stay here. No point both of us breaking our necks.'

The number of times she put herself out for these kids! One of these days she'd do it once too often.

'Thanks, Miss.' The boy beamed back. 'You're a star.'

'Tell me your name before I go,' she said, unlocking the door of the passenger side and slinging everything inside. 'I'm assuming that you have labelled your PE bag?'

He was smart in his school blazer beneath his parka coat, and the regulation school shoes he was wearing suggested that this boy had a mum who would expect to wash his kit at the end of every week. Very likely he was just as scared of getting into trouble with her as with the PE staff.

'John Smith, Miss,' he said.

'Well, that's easy enough to remember,' she said, shutting the car door and locking it. 'Right then. I'll see you in five minutes.'

Once again, she dodged the potholes as she retraced her steps back to the school building. Ed Robinson came out of the PE office in his outdoor clothes just as she was about to knock. The arrogant so-and-so.

They'd had a bit of a run-in the previous week regarding his timekeeping. All of the Year Seven boys had arrived at her lesson late because he'd gone over time. She'd been furious because she'd planned a very busy lesson which she now wouldn't be able to get through, thanks to Ed Robinson's belief that sport was more important than English.

He'd apologised, of course, but she hadn't believed a word of it.

'Oh,' she said. 'You.'

'Can I help?' he asked.

He didn't look at her as he spoke — all his attention appeared to be centred on the banana he was peeling. She wondered how much concentration it could take to remove the skin from a piece of fruit.

When she explained her purpose, he appeared, annoyingly, to be amused and suggested they went together to retrieve this boy's bag. Two pairs of eyes had to be better than one, he said. By the time they'd reached the boys' changing room, he'd eaten the banana and casually tossed the skin in a convenient bin.

'Right. You take one side and I'll take the other,' he said, pushing the door open.

The odour of boys' feet and cheap body spray assaulted her nostrils.

'You get used to it,' he said, hearing her gasp. 'Though it takes a while.'

He grinned, obviously enjoying her discomfort.

'Right,' he said. 'Find anything on your side?'

Julia peered underneath the benches along the length of one wall. There were indeed items of clothing lurking under there, but even had there happened to be a convenient bargepole nearby, she would have had no intention of retrieving them.

'Nothing here, either,' Ed said. 'What did you say the boy's name was again?'

'John Smith,' she said. 'Year Seven from the size of him. He said he had PE last lesson.'

'That doesn't sound right.' Ed Robinson scratched his head. 'Year Eleven were in here last period. I taught them myself.'

'Well, I'm not making it up,' she bristled. 'He's waiting by my car. In the overflow car park. Come with me if you don't believe me.'

'I intend to,' he said.

She was seized by a strong urge to punch him in the stomach. But from the look of those abs, he probably wouldn't even have felt it.

'So, where is he, then?' Ed Robinson asked when, after stumbling their way back in the dark, they finally reached the spot where she was parked.

Julia peered about her. There was no sign of John Smith anywhere.

'Did you leave the car door open?'

She thought hard. No, she definitely remembered locking it, she told him defensively.

'Well, in that case your John Smith, or whoever he is, appears to have broken in.'

Ed Robinson sounded very matter-of-fact considering the circumstances. He had his phone out now, observing the damage by its faint light.

'What? You're joking!'

'Wish I was. Looks like he got in by picking the lock with a screwdriver,' he said.

'But he's just a kid,' she said. 'How would he know about breaking into cars?'

Now Ed was flashing his phone about inside the car. Did anything ever faze him? she wondered.

'I think you should come and take a look,' he said. 'See if there's anything missing.'

Not knowing what to expect, but fearing the worst, she decided to take his advice. At first glance everything seemed just as she'd left it.

'Well, that's a relief! My radio's still intact, thank God!' she said. 'Ditto the shopping I did at lunch time.'

'Are you sure there's nothing missing?'

She peered closer. Actually, on closer inspection maybe there was a gap where there shouldn't have been one. She racked her brains trying to work out what had been there.

'It's like that party game, with a tray

and a tea towel and you have to remember what's been taken away, you know the one?' She was suddenly aware of how very foolish she must sound.

'Think,' he added. 'CDs? DVDs? Books?'

Julia stifled a scream. Not books. No. Not books exactly.

'Year Eleven's coursework!' The words came out like a strangled moan. 'My folders. They're gone.'

★   ★   ★

He told her that she'd had a shock and was in no fit state to drive. Now he was in the driver's seat, driving her home.

'What am I going to do?' she whispered, as implication piled upon implication.

No folders meant that she'd have nothing to present at tomorrow's meeting. A list of marks that she could pull down from her computer wouldn't be nearly enough evidence for the examiner.

The Board had a nasty habit of recalling all folders where the grade fell between borders. To her certain know-ledge at least seventy per cent of her class straddled the C/B border. The examiner would want to see them all and she would be able to show him none.

'This is a nightmare,' she breathed, as the car pulled up outside her door.

'Let's get this shopping in.'

Ed leaned across her to grab the bags from the back seat. He smelled pleasantly fresh, even at the end of a long school day.

'Good. You've got wine,' he said as the unmistakable chink of bottles rubbing up against each other rang out.

He couldn't possibly think she was going to ask him in to share it, could he?

'Door key?' He did.

Despite herself, she handed it over. She didn't know why she was acting like a damsel in distress. Perhaps it was because Ed Robinson was treating her like one.

'Here,' she said gruffly. 'Give me one of those bags.'

'No. It's fine.' He was already striding ahead of her towards her front door, a shopping bag in each hand.

'No, it's not fine. It's my shopping. Give me a bag,' she snapped.

He handed one over. The heaviest bag.

'You're stressed,' he said. 'Understandably. As soon as we get inside, I'll make you a cup of tea.'

'No. I'll make you a cup of tea,' she said, determined to have no more of this little woman business. Tea was just about admissible, she decided. But absolutely no wine.

Her tiny rented house was just as she'd left it that morning. A mess. Ed Robinson set about unpacking her shopping while she stood around looking like a spare part.

'I overslept,' she said, determined not to apologise for the crumbs on the bread board and the breakfast dishes neither washed nor put away.

It was when she remembered that it was because she'd overslept that she'd ended up in the car park with no security that she slumped down in the nearest chair and sank her head in her hands.

'All that work,' she groaned. 'Practically two years of their little lives. How am I going to explain it to them?'

It was going to be bad enough explaining it to Nev, her Head of Department. But it was going to be an even worse nightmare explaining it to the kids. Only this afternoon she'd handed back an excellent piece of work to Abbie Little, who'd struggled all through school with English because of her dyslexia.

Abbie had worked harder than anyone, doing draft after draft after draft, often staying behind to make sure that she was on the right lines with something. Kids like her were a joy to teach and she wasn't the only one in the class who had been determined to get the best possible grade they could.

'What say we swerve the tea and open the wine?' Ed said.

Alcohol never solved any problem. But what the heck! Her steely resolution to make him just one cup of tea before sending him on his arrogant, puffed-up way immediately melted at the suggestion.

When she removed her head from her hands, she saw Ed was staring at a bit of paper that must have fallen out of one of the shopping bags.

In that moment, anger replaced desperation. Damn cheek! Reading her receipts. Would he be taking her to task later for overspending? She should have changed her mind about the wine, but needs must.

'I'll get the wine glasses,' she said coldly, making sure he saw her disapproval.

Now they sat in the living room at either end of the settee, the bottle on the coffee table between them.

'I suppose I should report this to the police,' Julia said, after the first sip of wine.

'You might want to read this first,' Ed said.

Gingerly, she took the scrappy piece of paper from his hand. It wasn't the receipt for her shopping, after all. It was a note. And immediately she read it, she knew she was sunk.

Don't report this to the police. I know about you and Seth Ongondo, it said.

She tossed the rest of her wine down

her throat at breakneck speed. The alcohol sent her brain and her stomach on a collision course.

'This is all connected, isn't it? John Smith, whoever he is, the break-in, the files and this Seth Ongondo,' Ed commented. Julia slumped back in her seat.

'Why don't you tell me about him?' Irritatingly, his face was all concern.

Where did she start? Begin at the beginning, was what she said to students when they came to her either for advice or to justify their part in some shared misdemeanour. But when it came to Seth Ongondo, where was the beginning?

Four years ago, maybe, when he'd first arrived at the school, with barely a word of English? He'd been allocated to her tutor group and on that first morning at registration he'd been sitting all on his own, wearing a blazer with too short arms and — as she discovered when he stood up — trousers so short they flapped around his ankles.

How vulnerable he'd looked to her — a tall, lanky boy. His odd appearance and the fact that he was unable to defend himself verbally made it inevitable, she thought, that he'd be a target for bullies, and from the outset Julia had made it her mission to take Seth under her wing.

But to her surprise, her assumptions were wrong. What he initially lacked in verbal skills he more than made up for in the knack he had for making friends. And he was soon to prove himself gifted in other ways, too — as a linguist and a mathematician.

'Have you come across Seth at all?' Julie asked Ed.

'I don't teach him,' he said. 'But I've heard about him. And from how you describe him, I think I've seen him around. My height. Not so skinny now, either. Year Twelve, isn't he?'

She nodded.

'Got into some kind of trouble with the law, didn't he?'

Julia nodded again. Seth's precociously manly build may have explained in part why things went the way they did for him, she said. If he'd been smaller, perhaps he'd have stuck with friends in his own year. But from the start, he seemed drawn to the bigger boys who were of his own ethnicity — Kenyan. And the feeling was mutual.

'I'm guessing that all these boys feel there's safety in numbers,' she said. 'They're in the minority, after all, and the society they've adopted is not always on their side.'

'So if he's as bright as you say he is, how come he was stupid enough to get in trouble with the police?'

Julia felt suddenly angry with Ed.

'It's easy for you to say!' she said. 'A middle-class boy with every advantage.'

'You flatter me,' he said. 'My dad's a postman and my mum works part-time in the bookies. Which definitely makes me working class, I'd say.'

'Fair enough.' It was as near as he was going to get to an apology. 'But I don't expect you've ever lived anywhere like the Priory Estate.'

Ed sucked his teeth. The Priory Estate was notorious.

'That's where the council dumped him and his family then, is it?' he said. 'Welcome to England.'

18

She found herself nodding in agreement, like you would with a friend. Deciding to ignore the new bond that suddenly seemed to have formed between them, she continued with her story.

Seth Ongondo had made great strides academically, she said. Despite living in overcrowded conditions and being brought up by parents who spoke little English and who — due to the nature of the kind of jobs they were forced to do — were rarely there for Seth at the end of the school day.

His habit of mixing with the bigger boys and the fact that most of his free time was spent unsupervised soon led to some pretty unsavoury behaviour, which quickly began to escalate.

'What sort of behaviour?'

'No need to know the details. The usual. But after a run of it, they slapped an ASBO on him at the end of last year.'

She expected Ed to say something typical like, *Well, I guess it served him right.* Which it probably did. But, in fact, Ed said nothing. He just sat there and waited for the next bit.

'Seth wasn't like those other boys,' she said. 'He had hopes and dreams. I'd read about them in his essays. How he longed to go to university and get a degree. Make his parents proud. And I'd seen from his school reports just how capable he was of achieving that, too.'

She'd been staring at her hands, twisting them nervously as she spoke, but now she turned her gaze on Ed.

'You must think I'm very naïve,' she said. 'Putting all my faith in a boy like that.'

He didn't reply.

'When he came to tell me about the ASBO, he cried. He was just so ashamed,' she said. 'He was convinced it was the end of everything.'

Her head was beginning to throb, thanks to a combination of earlier events, the wine and no food, but she was determined to get to the hardest part of the story.

'But he got back on track really quickly.'

I'm turning over a new leaf, Miss, he'd said, when one day she stopped him in the corridor to say how proud she was of something she'd just heard about him from another teacher.

'This next bit's not so easy,' she said.

'Will this help?' Ed held up the wine bottle.

'Probably not,' she said. 'But go ahead anyway.' She held out her glass.

'One afternoon I was driving back from school after a bad day. I didn't want to come home straight away so I just drove around. Before I knew it I was practically on the edge of town. That was when I saw him. He was out of breath. Distressed. He'd obviously been running for a long time. So I offered him a lift. He said he'd be breaking his curfew if he didn't get home in half an hour. When I said I'd get him there and not to worry, he fell into the car, relieved.'

Seth's face had lit up. He seemed delirious with happiness. She'd read him the riot act, of course. Explained the implications and reminded him how fortunate he was that she happened to have been driving around just at the right time.

'When we got to his block, I stopped to let him out. That's when it happened.' She took a long slug of wine and savoured the effect. 'That's when he leaned over and kissed me.'

2

'He kissed you? Just like that? Out of the blue?'

'I didn't encourage him, Ed,' Julia protested. 'But after he got so upset about the ASBO, Seth got into the habit of stopping by my room most days after school and I'd invite him in.'

Immediately she could see how that might sound to a judge. A thirty-four-year-old woman and a sixteen-year-old boy getting cosy in the classroom after hours. Naivety didn't come into it.

'When I picked him up and drove him home that day, I swear I had no idea that he saw me as anyone other than a listening ear. We sat chatting in the car for a while outside his block of flats. I leaned across to open the passenger door and then he sort of lunged at me. It was hardly even a kiss. I jumped back. He apologised. I let him out and that was that. I put it down to sheer gratitude and youthful exuberance.

And now you know everything. I swear it's the truth.'

She had no idea why she'd felt the need to swear to him. Why should she care whether Ed Robinson believed her or not? Or that some kid was threatening to expose a non-existent fling with a pupil if she reported the theft of those wretched folders?

The answer came back immediately. Because even though none of it was true, it would definitely be investigated if there were even a hint of a rumour. And while that was happening she could say goodbye to her job. Not to mention having to watch the gutter press destroy her good name. Right now she needed all the friends she could get.

Ed appeared lost in thought. Finally he spoke.

'You know, women can have funny ideas about teenage boys,' he said.

She drew in her breath sharply. 'Have you heard one single thing I've said to you?' she said. Ed Robinson's brusque manner had always got on her nerves. She'd only let him drive her home out of desperation.

24

Hoisting herself up from the settee, she strode over to the window. The street outside was deserted.

'Thanks for bringing me back and everything,' she said stiffly. 'But it's getting late and you've probably got stuff to do.'

'Am I being dismissed, then?'

'Well, you've clearly made up your mind that I'm the Mrs Robinson of Dooley Park School.'

She could have sworn he'd just snorted. Spinning round, she glared at him.

'No! I didn't mean it in the way you think,' he said. 'Look, I'm sorry. For what it's worth, I believe you. But please, let me explain.'

'You've got sixty seconds.'

'What if Seth really does have feelings for you? Don't look so surprised! After all, you listened, supported him, believed in him. All that stuff is very flattering to a young boy.' What he said next came out in a rush. 'Plus you're a good-looking woman.'

Julia turned her back on him again and

began fiddling with the curtains.

'Don't be silly,' she squeaked.

'It's not a compliment,' Ed mumbled. 'Just a statement of fact.'

Now it was her turn to snort. 'Well, that's a relief,' she said mockingly.

Ed, suddenly subdued, changed the subject. She was grateful that he seemed unwilling to meet her eye as he spoke — it gave her time to compose herself.

'What if his pride's been hurt?' he said. 'Boys have a nasty habit of turning a story round for the purposes of self-preservation. Believe me, I know what I'm talking about.'

A wistful expression flitted across his face, presumably at the memory of his own cavalier youth. She imagined Ed Robinson would have been popular with the girls as a schoolboy. Those sporty kinds of boys usually were. Though never with her. Personally, she'd always been drawn to the pale, interesting types — the poets, the artists, the musicians.

Still was, actually, though they were thin on the ground in the circles she mixed in nowadays.

'What if he's told someone that you

made a pass at him? You know, to make him feel better about being spurned.'

She hated the idea that Seth would do something like that.

'He could easily have confided in a friend — your blackmailer, for instance — that you came on to him. I'm not saying he did,' he added, on seeing Julia's shocked expression. 'Just that he could. Or he could have told this friend the truth and this friend's just twisted it to make it into a more interesting story.'

She preferred the second theory, she said. People believed what they wanted to believe, in her experience. 'The truth comes in many guises,' she murmured.

'Is that Shakespeare?'

'No. Me, actually.'

They both grinned and the tension between them slackened.

'This John Smith. I can't believe he's the one who broke into my car and took those files, can you? There must have been a bigger boy involved. Seth's friend and confidant, I'm guessing.'

Ed agreed. The more he thought about it, the more convinced he was that John

Smith was simply a plant, put there just so she would fall for his story about a lost PE bag. And while she was away on her wild goose chase, the real culprit came along and helped himself to what he wanted.

But who was the real culprit? Julia suddenly realised she was starving. And when she was hungry she couldn't think.

'There's an Indian round the corner,' she said. 'You hungry?'

Ed nodded enthusiastically. 'Famished,' he said.

'Their chicken jalfrezi is to die for.'

'You like chicken jalfrezi?' Ed's face lit up.

'The hotter the better.'

'Bring a pen,' he said. 'We'll combine it with a brainstorming.'

By the time the popadoms had arrived, they'd already made a plan, written on a paper napkin. It went thus:

- Work out why anyone would want to take files in first place.
- Find out who John Smith is.
- Get name of boy he was aiding and abetting.

- Make a list of everyone whose folder was taken.
- Come up with a believable excuse as to why Julia is going to be turning up to cross-marking empty-handed tomorrow.

'It all looks a bit Famous Five, don't you think?' Julia said, glum still, despite the food and the beer.

Item number four on the list eclipsed all the others because it was the one she was going to have to deal with first, she added. Short of calling in sick, she could think of only one option: to explain the absence of folders with the truth. But if her blackmailer stuck to his guns and shopped her to the Principal, it was an option that was definitely closed to her.

'I think that shopping you to the Principal is going to be the least of your problems, actually,' Ed said.

'How do you mean?'

'This thing could go viral. He only needs to put something on his Facebook status and it could be all over the school in five minutes.'

Julia groaned. The Internet! Why hadn't she thought of that? Suddenly she'd lost her appetite.

'I'm sorry, Julia. I've panicked you when I should be helping you.'

'It doesn't matter,' she said. 'It's always as well to know what you're up against.'

He gave her an encouraging smile. Oddly, it made her feel just the tiniest bit better.

'So. This list then,' he said, pushing it across.

'Well, number three I can do here and now,' she said.

'Write the names down then.'

'No. You do it, please.' It all seemed suddenly hopeless.

She pushed the napkin towards him along with the pen. He was left-handed, she noticed, and his writing was awful. But in no time at all they had a list of names.

'Do you recognise any of these names?' Julia asked.

He shook his head.

'I see practically every boy in the school once or twice a week. Unless they're in any of the teams, it's impossible for me to recognise them just by their name. Now if they were all lined up in front of me . . . '

Julia sighed.

'I really am sorry,' he said. 'I want to get to the bottom of this just as much as you do.'

'And I'm grateful,' she said. 'But we're getting nowhere fast.'

When the main course arrived they sat in silence as the waiter set the various dishes down on the table.

'So,' Ed said, when he'd left. 'Any thoughts on number one on the list?'

Julia picked at her dish. 'What if there's something in one of those folders that they don't want me to see?' she said.

'I'm liking it. Something that could do them a lot of damage if it got into the wrong hands.'

There was nothing wrong with his appetite, she noticed.

'My hands, you mean?'

'Exactly.'

'Well, by that logic,' Julia said, 'he's just as scared of me as I am of him.'

His eyes met hers over a forkful of chicken.

'And the thing is, Julia, there are two of us and only one of him. And he's just a kid.'

* * *

Ah, man, this was stupid! Everything was such a mess.

The folders had taken over every surface of Jordan's bedroom now. If he was to stand up, there would be nowhere to put his feet that was paper-free. Spitting out a string of curses, he flung the folder he was holding over to the other side of the room. He watched as the contents unravelled and floated through the air before settling where they could.

Just one stupid bit of paper, that was all he was looking for. His client list. Rich geezers who wanted their drugs delivered discreetly, was the way Preston had described it. It's a big opportunity to turn your life around, Preston had said, once he'd handed over the list in return for the payment.

He'd had that list once. Danced around the living room with it, drinking her dad's whisky and wearing her dad's dressing gown. Him and Abbie, his gorgeous bird.

Every guy wants a girl like that. Smart, beautiful, rich. We're not rich really, she told him, when he'd commented on it that first time she'd let him come around and see where she lived. Not like millionaires or anything like that. Both her parents worked, she said. Long hours, weekends sometimes. Stupid jobs they got paid a ridiculous amount for.

Later, when the whisky and the joint had loosened her tongue, she told him she'd rather they spent more time with her than keep on giving her money and stuff. She'd cried a bit then and he'd comforted her. Then one thing had led to another, which he'd known it would because he'd had experience of girls crying before.

When his mobile rang, he jumped six feet in the air. It was that kid.

'How d'you get my number?' he snarled.

The boy wouldn't say.

'What do you want? Be quick. I'm busy.'

He said he was ringing up about the blazer. His mum had found it.

'Ah, man! Why d'you let her go and do that?'

It hadn't been deliberate, the kid said. The problem was his mother seemed to think she had a God-given right to poke about among his things.

'Look, kid. I don't want you ringing me again, right. Delete this number.'

The kid said he would, except first he wanted to know what to do about his mum. She was threatening to take it back to the school.

'Then stop her!'

He felt like screaming. Everything was getting worse and worse. He'd picked this kid because he'd needed somebody with a bit of a vocabulary and a brain. Big mistake, obviously. He would have been better off with one of the kids from the estate who could blag for England. The kid wanted to know how.

'How am I supposed to know that?' he exploded. 'Use your brains. But just remember, if anything gets back to me that you've been pointing the finger, then you'd better watch your back. OK?'

Before the kid could reply, he switched off his phone. As if he didn't have enough to contend with. Never mix business with pleasure, was the saying. It had to be a saying for a reason and he'd just discovered the reason for himself.

You've got to concentrate when you're working. You can't be drinking and smoking spliffs and messing about with women. He should have checked his pocket when he got home. Made sure that he'd picked it up off the floor where he'd been sprawled out next to her, trying to distract her. Abbie had got impatient with him. You have to wait, she said. I have to sort my work out first.

That's why he was so sure it had ended up there, in her file, after she'd stopped going on about her coursework and turned her mind to other, more interesting activities. That's why he'd had to break into that car and get the file back. Except it wasn't there. It wasn't in any of them.

He jammed his thumbnail in his mouth and started nibbling away at it like he always did when things got on top of him. It had to be with her. That teacher. She'd found it and was calling his bluff. Hoping he wouldn't let out what he knew about her goings-on with Seth. Testing him to see if he was man enough to act on all those secrets Seth had told him.

Teachers. He hated them. All his life they'd sneered at him like he was something stuck to the bottom of their shoes. Well, he'd show her. He wasn't giving up so easy. He wanted what was his. And he was going to get it.

★   ★   ★

Julia was sitting at her desk still praying for a miracle. It was a long time since lunch and so far no one in the English department had gone down with food poisoning, and a glance through the window at a clear blue sky suggested there was little chance of a monsoon either. To say that time was running out was an understatement.

'Coming, Julia? We're all waiting for you.'

Joan Bates, who'd been teaching English at Dooley Park since the year dot, had crept up on her in that creepy way she had and now stood at her shoulder. How did she move so silently? Julia wondered. Was she on castors? She glanced at Joan's feet. No, black lace-ups. She'd never imagined that Joan Bates had much of a life but right now she'd have swapped identities at the drop of a hat.

'Just grabbing myself a coffee!'

'Oh, there's no need.' Joan rubbed her thin hands together. They made a sound like rustling leaves. 'Coffee and tea's provided. Biscuits, too!' Her eyes lit up behind her glasses in anticipation.

'Brilliant!'

Julia struggled to sound convincing. The realisation that there wasn't going to be a miracle struck her with force as reluctantly she hoisted herself from her chair. The folders hadn't been returned to her desk and Ed, despite the reassurances of last night, when he'd dropped her off at her door, had as yet failed to come up trumps with a plan to get her out of the meeting.

She'd had a couple of texts from him — one to say that the only John Smith on the register was a six-foot tall, freckled redhead in Year Eleven, and a second, about half an hour ago, that had asked her how she was. She'd replied immediately with the words, *Plan? What plan?*

'Why don't you skip on ahead and tell everyone I'm on my way and . . . '

She didn't reach the end of her sentence, because in that moment the fire alarm set up a clamour that was loud enough to waken the dead. Oh, frabjous day, callooh, callay! A breathing space! The weight of the world suddenly lifted from her shoulders and she had to restrain herself from doing a little dance.

'Oh, my goodness.' Joan pressed her hands to her ears. 'No one said anything about a drill! How inconvenient!'

Julia, copying Joan, nodded in vehement agreement. But there was no time to be lost, she mouthed. Other members of staff were already leaving the staffroom. They needed to get to their stations and check that the children in their respective forms were all present and correct.

With a thudding heart, Julia joined everyone else, staff and pupils alike, in the noisy mass exodus to the sports field, the designated meeting point for everyone in case of fire. It was cold outside and Julia had forgotten her jacket in the rush, but the relief she felt at having been given some breathing space more than made up for any physical discomfort.

Silently, she applauded Ed for coming up with such a genius solution. She was almost jubilant when finally they were allowed back inside. Thanks to students mucking around, it had taken far longer than it should to assemble everyone, and even after they'd counted all present and correct there was another long wait while the fire marshals went inside to check that it was safe to return.

'I really don't know if we can get through everything we need to get through in the time we have left,' she overheard Head of English, Nev Ferguson, remark to Joan on the way back inside. 'I have another meeting later this evening and since I'm chairing I can't possibly be late.'

Keeping him in her eye line, which

wasn't hard as he was about six foot four and had the loudest voice of anyone she knew, she put a spurt on, quickly catching them up.

'I hope you don't think I was eavesdropping, Nev, but I couldn't help overhearing,' she said. 'If you'd rather leave it till next week, I for one . . . '

Ed was hanging around outside the staffroom door, as the three of them hurried past on their way to the room where the English meeting was scheduled to be held.

'Thank you,' she mouthed silently.

He raised his eyebrows, seemingly surprised. She thought she saw him reach for his phone as he disappeared from view once they'd rounded the corner and left him behind. When she heard her own phone bleep a message outside the meeting room, she knew she'd guessed right.

If she'd been looking inside the room, like Nev and Joan and the other members of the team who'd chosen just that moment to pull up behind them, she would have witnessed the exact same scene that they all witnessed.

But she was looking at Ed's text. *I didn't do it* — it read — *I thought it was you!*

And so there was a delay before their collective cries and yells reached her. She understood the situation soon enough, however, when Nev's booming voice said, 'The folders. Someone's taken them. Every single one!'

3

Nev Ferguson, Head of English, advanced on the classroom like a wary explorer. Julia could have sworn he actually sniffed the air.

'They were all here. Set out in piles. Waiting to be cross-marked,' he yelled.

Not to be outdone in the histrionics stakes, Joan Bates, who'd been teaching English at the school since the year dot, immediately launched herself at each cupboard door in turn, tugging them open and rifling through the contents, like a small foraging mammal. Julia fully expected her to start ripping up the floorboards next.

The two youngest members of the English department, Ellie Grey and Jim Harper, were far too cool to allow themselves to get flustered by anything. They watched the proceedings from the doorway with a languid air. When they suggested it was a harmless prank and that they shouldn't overreact, Julia quickly decided to back them up.

'Absolutely!' she agreed. 'If we start panicking, it'll be all round the school how easily we've been had. We'll never live it down. I bet you any money they'll all be back in place again tomorrow anyway. I vote we all go home.'

Joan Bates disagreed. The consequences of the theft of these folders would be catastrophic, she insisted. How on earth were they going to explain it to the Board?

As a department, she reminded them, they were legally obliged to submit a list of thoroughly cross-checked marks by the end of next week, as well as being expected to send off any individual folders, too, should a request be made to that effect.

Julia was filled with a sudden urge to strangle the woman. Not least because, infuriatingly, Joan had right on her side. The repercussions of the loss of every single GCSE folder were indeed unimaginable. Not only would they have the education authorities on their backs, but the parents would be up in arms, and as for the students who'd done the work only to lose it — well, riots would be the least of it!

Speaking personally, of course, whoever had done this had done Julia a massive favour. Now hers wasn't the only pile missing.

'What do you think we should do, Nev?' Joan only ever took Nev's opinion into consideration on anything. The word sycophantic could have been coined for her.

Julia held her breath. She happened to glance in Jim Harper's direction, simply because he was nearest the door through which she longed to escape. He rolled his eyes at her dramatically.

'I think Julia's right,' Nev said, after a theatrical pause worthy of the hammiest thespian.

Joan gasped, Julia gulped, Jim yawned and Ellie, typically, tossed her blonde hair.

'The power of the Internet knows no bounds these days, alas,' he went on. 'We must not be made a laughing stock by being tweeted and twittered about.'

Nev wasn't altogether au fait with modern communication methods, but even so, Julia appreciated his support.

'But we should at least report it.' Joan, nostrils flaring and cheeks aflame, was not going down without a fight.

Nev considered her words. Did she really think that was such a good idea? he said, once he'd chewed them over. After all, they'd left the folders unattended. Something the Principal might consider a lapse of security on their part. Personally, he was inclined to think that the fewer people who knew about this, the better.

Julia watched with interest as the dawning light of understanding flickered over Joan's face.

'Now you've explained it like that, it makes sense,' she said. 'Time enough to report it to the Principal when the files fail to turn up once we've had a good look round for them.'

She smiled at them all encouragingly. Everyone nodded vigorously in response, none more so than Julia.

'I'm sure it won't come to that,' she

said, surprised at how sure of herself she sounded, given she had absolutely nothing to base her hopes on.

'Good! Then I suggest we all get here early tomorrow and hold a rigorous search,' Nev said. 'Eight o'clock all right with everyone?'

More breathing time at least, Julia thought. And more time to collar Ed to see if he had any more idea than she did about what the heck was going on.

* * *

Ed was outside the gym deep in conversation with a bunch of burly boys in tracksuits. When he saw her, he dismissed them before scuttling over towards her.

'So, who do you think set the alarm off then, if you didn't and I didn't either? I'm totally mystified,' he hissed.

'You'll be even more mystified when you hear this,' Julia said.

'I don't get it,' he said, once she'd filled him in on the most recent events.

'You and me both, mate,' she said.

'Look, we can't talk here.'

They strode towards the main exit in contemplative silence. As they approached the entrance area, a tall black woman was peering through the sliding window that gave access to the receptionist.

Julia took in the woman's striking appearance — the hair, the heels, the statement bag and the smart suit — in one glance. How did some women manage to pull that co-ordinated, professional yet damned sexy look together in the morning and make it last all day? she thought enviously.

'Lakisha!'

Ed had stopped in his tracks at the sight of her, clearly flustered.

'Ed! Hi!'

Now it was the woman's turn to acknowledge Ed, which she did with a reserved manner that bordered on the chilly. Julia wondered if perhaps she ought to make herself scarce, but curiosity got the better of discretion.

'What are you doing here? I thought Darius was at St Xavier's?' Ed said.

'Yeah, that's right.'

'So. How's he getting on there? Does he like it?'

Darius? St Xavier's? Ed seemed very familiar with this lady's family history. A small itch of jealousy suddenly flared up inside her, seizing her by surprise.

'It's about Darius I'm here, actually, Ed. I wanted to return this.'

Julia had already spotted the plastic carrier bag bearing the name of everyone's favourite posh supermarket that Lakisha had been clutching. She immediately deducted points for this small lapse of sartorial taste.

'I found it while I was cleaning Darius's room.' Lakisha held up the school blazer she'd extracted from the bag for them to see, her lips curling in distaste. 'He said he found it in the park.'

'Kids these days, eh? I bet his mum's been turning the house upside down looking for it,' Julia said.

'I know I would,' Lakisha replied shortly, registering her presence for the first time. 'I was going to drop it off at Reception here on my way back home from work,' she said. 'But it seems like

48

whoever's job it is to deal with parent enquiries has got more important things to do.'

Julia followed Lakisha's gaze. On the window was taped a notice. *Due to personal problems there is no one on reception this afternoon*, it read. She'd been ringing on and off all day but had only got an answer machine. Not something that would ever happen at St Xavier's, apparently.

'I'm sure the receptionist wouldn't have taken the afternoon off for no reason,' Julia said defensively.

Lakisha obviously didn't think much to this explanation.

'Well, you may as well have this then.' She held out the blazer with disdain.

'Thank you,' Julia said. 'It was very thoughtful of you to return it.'

'I've checked for a name inside already,' Lakisha said, as Julia did the same thing. 'There is none. It wouldn't happen at St Xavier's. Name tapes are obligatory at my son's school.'

Julia refrained from saying that so was forking out thirty thousand quid a year to buy a place.

'I'm sure we'll find a home for it, won't we, Mr Robinson?' she said, turning to Ed.

'What? Oh, yes. I'm sure we will.' What was the matter with Ed? Julia wondered. He appeared to be in a trance.

Lakisha returned the now empty carrier to her own bag. Then, hitching the strap up on to her shoulder, she smiled.

'Well, nice seeing you again, Ed,' she said, proffering her cheek for a kiss. 'And you too, Miss . . . er . . . '

'Yes,' Julia said, observing the mealy-mouthed peck Ed planted on Lakisha's cheek with relish. 'You too.'

'Wow!' she said, as Lakisha disappeared through the exit.

Ed sighed. The release of tension was palpable.

'Please. Don't ask,' he said. 'Just let's find a pub. You're going to need a drink once you hear this.'

* * *

Once they were seated in the snug of The White Horse, the local watering hole where staff members from Dooley Park repaired to after a stressful day, Ed finally spoke.

'It was Darius,' Ed said. 'The boy you saw at your car. Lakisha's son. I've been thinking about it all the way here and telling myself it can't be true but, of course, it must be.'

'What?' Julia didn't think she was hearing straight. 'He's the little boy who sent me off on that wild goose chase and stood guard while someone broke into my car?'

Ed nodded glumly.

'Look,' she said, 'you're going to have to help me out here. For a start, what exactly is your relationship with this Lakisha?'

Ed sat hunched over his beer, grasping it between both hands and staring into it as if it were a crystal ball.

'She's an ex,' he said simply.

'Oh. OK.'

'We met in a bar. I couldn't believe my luck at first,' he said. 'A great-looking woman like that coming on to me.'

'Is this where I'm meant to say that

you're talking rubbish and that any woman would be proud to be seen with you?' she said.

'I'm flattered.' His face relaxed into a smile.

'Don't be,' she said. 'It's just a line. Now continue.'

He smiled again. They had seen each other a few times, he went on. She seemed like a regular kind of girl. Then she invited him back to her house for Sunday lunch.

'When I turned up, the flat was full of people in their Sunday best from her church,' he said. 'All waiting to meet me. It brought me out in a cold sweat, I don't mind telling you.'

'And that's when you legged it?' she said, amused.

'I wish I had,' he said. 'But I stayed. I probably felt it would have been impolite not to. And when I got invited to church the following week and back to someone else's house for lunch with Lakisha and her kid, she made it impossible for me to say no by accepting on my behalf. That was what she was like. Controlling.'

She ran her own business; she organised church events; she brought up her son single-handed. She was successful in every area but one, Ed said glumly. She lacked a husband and her son lacked a father.

'It was like she'd marked me out as the one,' he said, tracing quotation marks in the air.

Julia snorted.

'Don't laugh,' he said. 'It was frightening.'

'How did you manage to extricate yourself from the situation, then?'

'I finally texted her after another two months of hymns and Sunday lunches. Said I wasn't ready to commit. She didn't even reply. Shows how broken-hearted she was. Today's the first time I've spoken to her since that day.'

Julia admired his honesty and couldn't help feeling some sympathy for the poor man. But she wasn't satisfied that she knew the whole story.

'Why did you let it go on for so long?' she asked him.

'Darius,' he said. 'I felt sorry for him, poor little blighter. He was such a bright spark. But his life was all church and homework. Not surprising he's got mixed up in this business with your car and everything?'

'You think he's rebelling?'

'Stands to reason,' Ed said.

'We don't know for sure that it's him yet,' Julia said.

Ed gave her a look. 'It's him,' he said. 'Come back to my place and I'll see if I've got a snap of him somewhere.'

'We're going to have to go and pay him a visit, you do realise that, don't you?' Julia was deadly serious.

'Are you kidding? And tell his mother what? That her precious son is probably best buddies with a villain, standing guard while a teacher's car was broken into?'

'Yes, if necessary!'

'No. I can't do it.'

'Can I remind you what's at stake?' she said. 'Someone is blackmailing me because of an incident with a pupil that could make me look very dodgy and possibly lose me my job, even though I am the innocent party. And now, not content with whipping one set of files out of my car, they've succeeded in nicking the whole damn lot.'

'I know. But I can't. He's not a bad lad. Just bored and looking for excitement. If we go round there and tell her what he's been up to, she'll bring the whole wrath of her church down on him. Poor kid's life won't be worth living.' Ed sank back in his seat, clearly distraught.

They sat in silence, each locked into their own thoughts. It suddenly occurred to Julia that they had more in common than she could possibly ever have imagined.

'We're both as bad as each other,' she said. 'You defending Darius, me defending Seth.'

'It had occurred to me.'

'So what are we going to do?'

Ed's hand was edging ever closer to hers. She kept hers in exactly the same place. When it finally disappeared, beneath his, it was as if all the tension of these last few days ebbed right away.

'We could go back to your place,' she said, keeping her voice level. 'Didn't you say you might have a picture of Darius? Then we can decide what to do next.'

'I think that sounds like a brilliant idea,' he said.

★ ★ ★

'And now at six-thirty, it's time for the local news. The body of a young black male has been found in wasteland near . . . '

Julia stuck out her left arm and groped around for where her radio alarm should have been. It took a moment before she remembered that she hadn't slept in her own bed last night.

The radio went suddenly silent as Ed, over on the other side of the bed, made a sudden lunge towards it, before turning over and sliding towards her.

'Whose idea was it to put the alarm on for six-thirty?' he groaned as he took her in his arms. 'Tell me it was a joke and we can both go back to sleep.'

Julia kept her eyes shut tight. She'd dreaded this moment — waking up with Ed at her side. It was a mistake. She knew it and he probably knew it, too. The best thing to do in these circumstances, she decided, was to play it cool.

Hurriedly jumping out of bed and grabbing her underclothes, she reminded him why the alarm had gone off so early. She had no clean clothes and she had to be at school for eight to help look for the missing folders. A waste of time, as they'd both agreed, but she had no choice but to play the game. She could ill afford to draw attention to herself by not showing up or showing willing.

'Today is going to be an awful day,' she sighed, wishing she could stay exactly where she was till the whole thing blew over.

'You're right. It's going to be hell,' Ed said, as he stretched out his muscular frame. 'But first things first. Are you a coffee or a tea person?'

★　★　★

Julia was making her way to her classroom where her Year Eleven GCSE set would be waiting for her. Considering what she was about to confess to them, she felt ridiculously calm.

Perhaps it helped that she wouldn't be the only member of the English team going through the same torture. They were all in it together.

Abbie Little was on her phone outside the classroom with a face like thunder. 'Pick up, pick up, pick up,' she muttered over and over at her phone.

'Switch it off now, please, Abbie, and come inside,' Julia said.

Abbie kissed her teeth. Where did she learn to do that, Julia wondered, not without admiration, particularly as she'd never got the hang of it herself. She could have hauled the girl over the coals for it, actually, except she didn't have the energy, being far too preoccupied with how she was going to get through the next ten minutes without being lynched.

Though as soon as she crossed the threshold, she realised she didn't even have ten minutes. The news had already filtered through via text messages from friends in other sets who'd already been informed that they were going to have to do their four coursework pieces all over again, which was the decision the English team had made — albeit with heavy hearts — after a thorough search of the premises had revealed that the English files were nowhere to be found.

She decided the best strategy was to shut her ears to shrieks of horror, cries of disbelief and — by far in the majority — displays of cussed defiance. Raising both hands, she called for quiet. It came sooner than she had anticipated, making her realise that there was not one young person in this room who wasn't genuinely anxious. She suddenly realised how much she loved them all.

She didn't go into details. Briefly, she said, someone had pulled a ridiculous stunt and run off with all their coursework files while they'd all been lining up outside when the fire alarm went off. It stank, but the situation wasn't insurmountable.

Everyone had backed up their work, she knew, because she'd overseen it herself. The only piece of coursework they were going to have to do again was the one handwritten piece the Board still insisted upon as evidence that in these days of word processing the candidate could actually write.

'Think of it as an opportunity to improve your mark,' she said encouragingly, smiling through the collective groan that greeted this statement.

It was going far better than she'd anticipated, actually. Until at least half a dozen students raised their hands and said they'd lost their memory sticks, so no longer had back-up copies.

When Julia calmly reiterated that in that case they were going to have to start all over again, all hell broke loose, which she could have predicted. She was relieved when the bell rang. Though most of those students with no memory sticks had been co-operative, some were resistant to any offers of extra help, one or two even threatening legal action.

Now she was alone. Or so she thought. Abbie Little had crept back into the classroom. She hovered by the door, looking woebegone.

'I need to speak to you, Miss,' she said.

'What is it, Abbie? You're not going to tell me you've lost your memory stick, too, I hope?'

'It's worse than that,' she said, shaking her head.

Julia braced herself. Abbie on the phone to some unknown boy. Pick up, pick up, pick up. A pregnancy scare was all they needed right now.

'Well, you can tell me, surely?' Julia said. 'I won't bite.'

Tears spilled from Abbie's eyes. 'It's the alarm, Miss,' she said. 'It was me who set it off. And then I took those folders out of the room and hid them.'

4

Anxious that they may be overheard by passing staff or students, Julia swiftly manoeuvred Abbie outside. Now, in the relative privacy of her car, she struggled to digest not only Abbie's confession — that she'd been responsible for setting off the alarm and taking the other files — but also the reason her car had been broken into. Abbie's boyfriend, Jordan, had done it because it contained something very important to him.

'It's a list of people who want to buy drugs, Miss,' she said, clearly very anxious. 'He bought it from someone called Preston for a lot of money. He said it was a business investment and he was going to make a fortune.'

Julia was horrified. 'How ever did you get involved with someone like that, Abbie?'

Abbie hung her head. 'I was stupid, Miss,' she said.

'And why on earth did you agree to help him by taking those other folders?'

'He didn't ask me to do any of that,' Abbie said. 'That was my idea. I did it for you, Miss.'

'For me?'

'I thought that if all the other files went missing, too, it would look like they'd all disappeared together and you wouldn't have to explain the real story.'

'So he's spun you that stupid tale about Seth and me as well?' Julia was exasperated. 'It's not true, Abbie,' she said.

'I know that,' Abbie said. 'It's just stupid boys' talk.'

'I haven't got his client list. End of. I can't produce it out of thin air,' she said.

'He thinks you have got it and you're just holding out. He says you're making a fool of him.' Abbie's voice began to shake with fear. 'But that you won't succeed.'

Julia was shaking too now. With fury.

'And he says that unless he gets the list by lunchtime tomorrow he's going to carry out his threat.'

Tears began to spill from Abbie's eyes.

'He's going to put everything on Facebook that you did — that he says Seth says you did — so that everyone will be able to read it.'

Julia transferred her fury from Jordan to Seth. After everything she'd done to help him, too.

At her side, Abbie alternately sobbed, sniffed and apologised. She was bound to have a tissue in her bag, Julia thought, reaching over to grab it from the back seat. But no amount of scrabbling inside it revealed one. She tried the side pocket next to her, but all it brought forth was sweet wrappers.

In desperation, she tugged open the drawer by the steering wheel. Out tumbled a packet of tissues and an empty plastic bottle that had once contained water. Something else fell out, landing in the cramped space between them. Abbie saw it, too. Immediately, she stopped crying.

'Oh my God, Miss,' she said. 'That's it! It's Jordan's list.'

She bent down to retrieve it, but Julia was quicker. It was the water bottle that suddenly triggered her memory. Now it came back to her! She'd crammed it into the drawer along with that scrappy bit of paper! She remembered thinking it must have fallen out of someone's file and that it might be important to someone, so she'd better put it somewhere safe until she had time to work out who it belonged to.

'Aren't you going to give it to me, Miss, so I can give it back?'

'No, Abbie, I don't think I am, actually,' Julia said.

Curious to see more of this list, she ran her eyes down the page. One name sprang out at her. No, surely not! But she couldn't think about that just now.

'Tell him from me that if he wants his list, he's going to have to talk to me direct. Not through a messenger,' she said.

'Yes, Miss,' Abbie said timidly.

'There are plenty of nice boys out there, Abbie. It's not all about being cool, you know.'

Abbie looked suitably shamefaced. Julia decided not to embarrass the girl further.

She'd get there in the end, she was sure. Maybe every girl needed a brush with a boy like Jordan some time in their life, just to get danger out of their system.

'Look! Everyone's going back inside after break.' Julia reached for the door handle. 'I think we should do the same, don't you?'

Abbie nodded. 'But what are you going to do with the list? Give it to the police? Because you know what will happen if you do.'

'No, I'm not going to go to the police. Not for now, anyway. I'm going to wait for Jordan to get in touch with me again and I'm going to do a bit of thinking, too.'

She leaned across to let Abbie out. 'And if you've got any sense, you'll do the same.'

★   ★   ★

Immediately she was back inside, Julia got on her phone to Ed. She actually had a free period now, so she could have sought him out and made the attempt to speak to

66

him in person. But she felt safer at a distance. She could say what she had to say and move on without reading any meaning into the way he looked at her or — worse — chose not to.

Oh, God! Relationships were so complicated. All this game-playing. Trying not to be the idiot who showed their hand first. But it had to be done. She had her pride, after all.

Ed's phone went straight to voicemail. Had he switched it off deliberately when her name flashed up on to his screen? Did he regret spending the night with her? Believing that if she didn't leave a message she would come across as desperate and pathetic, she went ahead.

'I've got the piece of paper. And I know who took the files. I'm meant to wait for him to contact me. But I've decided not to. So we need to make a visit to your little friend Darius and see if he knows how we can contact this boy before I end up on Facebook. Time's running out, so get back to me asap,' she said.

Darius was the son of a woman Ed used to be involved with. It was Darius who'd helped Jordan break into Ed's car.

One of Julia's colleagues, Ellie Grey, was hurrying down the corridor, looking miserable. Julia snapped her phone shut and greeted her.

'Ellie, what's the matter?'

'Have you heard about Sharon's nephew, Preston?'

'Sharon the receptionist, you mean?'

'Yes. The poor boy's been murdered,' she said. 'Stabbed.'

'No! When? Have they found out who did it?'

Ellie shook her head. 'All I know is that he went missing a couple of days ago. Sharon must have known about it because she went home yesterday, remember?'

Julia did. The lovely Lakisha — Ed's ex-girlfriend — had complained that such dereliction of duty for mere *personal problems* wouldn't have been countenanced at St Xavier's, where her darling son Darius went to school.

'And then I heard something on the news this morning about a body being found,' she went on.

'I heard that, too.'

'Seventeen years old. Can you imagine?' She sniffed back a tear. 'Did you ever teach him, Julia? He left before I came, of course. Preston Masters, he was called.'

Julia said she hadn't taught him. But it didn't stop her from being affected by the news. There would be staff at the school who had, plus he must have more relatives here among the pupils, besides his aunt.

Her phone beeped a message. 'I'd better get that,' she said.

'And I'd better get to my lesson,' Ellie said. 'Though how I'm ever going to get them to concentrate on their work now this has come out, I've no idea.'

'Don't try,' she said. 'Just let them talk. That's what I'd do.'

'I will, then,' Ellie said. 'Maybe it will help.'

Julia stood there and pondered the dreadful news, watching Ellie make her troubled way down the corridor. Then she headed for the staffroom. At her desk she read Ed's message.

St Xavier's Under-12's playing here

tonight. Darius in team. We'll nab him then, it said. Talk about serendipity!

'Glad to see you've got time to waste on your mobile phone.'

Julia almost jumped out of her chair. Joan had done her usual trick of silently creeping up behind her.

'You've heard the news about that boy,' she said.

'Terrible,' she said. 'Poor Sharon. Her family must be absolutely devastated. Now, if you don't mind . . . '

But Joan was going nowhere. She'd been thinking about the missing files, she said, leaning up against the empty desk opposite Julia's. And something just kept bothering her.

'Oh?'

It was very strange, Joan said, but she was certain that Julia's files hadn't been there with the others in the classroom when they'd gone missing.

'You were late and I came out to find you,' she said. 'Remember? And then the fire alarm went off and we all went outside. Then when we came back in we found the files had gone. Except yours hadn't been there in the first place.'

'What are you suggesting, Joan?' Julia kept her voice even.

'I'm not suggesting anything, Julia,' she said. 'It's probably just my memory.'

'That can happen,' Julia said, flourishing her trump card. 'Too much marijuana, I'd say.'

Joan went white. 'What are you saying?' she hissed.

Julia smiled. 'Nothing, Joan. I'm very good at keeping secrets, as I trust you are, too.'

Joan looked shaken, as well she might. Thanks to Jordan's list, Joan's name and address had been revealed to her as one of his clients.

* * *

It was lunchtime and Abbie lay in wait for Seth Ongondo, who she guessed would be coming out of the Sixth Form Block any minute now. She was still smarting from Miss's obvious disappointment in her for choosing Jordan as a boyfriend.

Miss was right. He was scum. She didn't

trust him an inch. Even if he got that list back, what was to stop him posting those lies on Facebook, anyway? Or worse, coming to blackmail Miss again about them?

Now she was determined to get back in her good books. She was going to dump Jordan and she was going to get Seth to stop him posting that stuff about Miss on Facebook. When it came to a fight, she didn't fancy Jordan's chances against powerfully-built Seth, not for one second.

Here he came now. Everyone knew of Seth, even if they didn't know him personally. Most of the girls had a crush on him, but Abbie firmly believed he was out of her league. Anyway, she was off boys for the rest of her life.

'Oi — you!' She stood right in the middle of his path, arms planted on her hips.

'Hey,' he said, friendly enough. 'Do I know you?'

'You know Miss Sumner,' she said. 'And you're a friend of Jordan's.'

'Jordan? I don't think so.' Seth slowed to a stop. 'I don't hang around with that loser any more.'

What was all this about Miss Sumner? he wanted to know. Abbie told him everything from start to finish.

Seth's expression darkened. 'Oh, my days. He ain't going to get away with getting Miss into trouble. I owe her big time.'

'So it's all lies then?'

'OK, I kissed her. On the cheek. That bit was true. Because she got me out of trouble. But anything else? No way. She's a teacher, for one thing. And for another, she's old.'

'Don't say that,' Abbie said. 'Miss is lovely. And if we don't stop Jordan, he could end up getting her sacked and I won't get my GCSEs.'

Seth grinned. 'Well,' he said, 'we can't have that, can we?'

But what was her connection with Jordan? he wanted to know.

'A severed one,' she said.

She could see she'd properly impressed him with that line. And he'd properly impressed her, too. She thought he was proper gallant, coming to the aid of an older lady.

* * *

'Do you remember this woman, Darius?'

Darius, hair still damp from his post-match shower, peered anxiously up at her. Julia could hardly bear to be cruel.

'Because I remember you,' she said. 'John Smith, isn't it?'

'I'm sorry, Miss,' he said.

For protection, he edged closer to Ed, who'd had a word with his mate, the St Xavier coach, nabbed Darius and brought him back to the PE staffroom.

'This boy who broke into this lady's car — is he a friend of yours?' she asked him.

Darius shook his head violently. His younger sister was, he said. He'd asked her to guard the car for him, but she wouldn't, so Darius had volunteered. For a laugh.

'Not sure your mum would think it was a laugh,' Ed said. 'Or the people in your church.'

Darius looked angry.

'The police might not be so thrilled, either,' Ed said.

'You wouldn't tell them, would you?'

74

Ed shrugged. 'It's not up to me,' he said. 'It wasn't my car you broke into.'

'I won't do anything like this ever again, Miss. I promise.'

His brief display of bravado vanished. He turned his gaze towards her, a small, frightened boy once more.

'Come on.' Ed held out his hand and Darius took it. It was a gesture Julia found oddly touching. 'I'll walk you back to your coach,' he said.

'I've got Jordan's number,' he said, on his return. 'I'll text him. Tell him we need to talk. Darius said he was warned to delete it, but he didn't.'

'Does that kid ever do anything he's told?' Julia said.

Ed sighed. 'He's a great kid. He needs a father. I hope Lakisha manages to find the right one this time.'

'You look sad,' Julia said. 'Don't blame yourself for this.'

Ed looked at her for a long time. 'You're a very perceptive woman,' he said. 'Do you know that?'

And then she was in his arms and he was kissing her.

Jordan paced up and down the eight-by-eight box that was jokingly called his room and checked the message again.

Givin files back 2 Miss. Yur dumped.

How could Abbie do this to him? Didn't she know he was going into business for her, to make her proud of him?

When his phone sprang into life, he jumped. Seth. Long time no see! Perhaps he had some better news. He didn't.

'Word is, you're about to do something really stupid, even for you.' Seth's fury crackled down the phone. 'I'm telling you to forget it.'

Jordan bristled. He wasn't going to be pushed about by anybody. This was business, he said. Seth should just keep out of it. That teacher had something of his and unless he got it back . . .

'You heard about Preston?'

Already he knew this wasn't going to be good news.

'He's dead, Jordan. I just heard. Word is, he was trying to make a new start. And that he sold his client list on to some loser. Needed the money for a ticket out. Except once you're involved in that sort of business you can never escape.'

A cold ripple of fear ran through Jordan.

'Give it up, Jordan. You've lost your girlfriend. Don't lose your life.'

★　★　★

The atmosphere in the staffroom was bleak. The Principal had made the announcement that Preston Masters had been the unfortunate victim of a knife crime — probably drug related, according to the police.

He'd said he hoped that staff would use the opportunity to discuss with their students the pitfalls of getting involved in this kind of lifestyle. And now he wanted to see the English team in Nev's office.

It didn't look good. Complaints had been coming in thick and fast from parents and pupils alike, apparently, about the cavalier attitude of the English team who expected students to redo in one short week work that had taken them eighteen months to do in the first place.

Julia sat at her desk preparing herself for a thorough roasting. She was going to tell all, she decided. She had no intention of giving Jordan his client list back and being responsible for setting him off on a life of crime. Publish and be damned, as the saying went. No matter if it did mean the end of *her* career as well as his.

'Joan!' There she was again — the invisible woman.

'I want to say one thing and then I hope we never have to mention it again,' Joan hissed. 'I bought that marijuana for my neighbour. She has MS and occasionally the pain gets so bad it's the only thing that seems to relieve it.'

'I hear you, Joan.'

Well, that was another decision made. She knew what she had to do with Jordan's list now and she wouldn't be handing it over to the police. She was no fan of Joan's, but she had no intention of getting the poor woman locked up for trying to be a Good Samaritan.

'Come on, we'd better get this meeting

over and done with,' she added, grabbing her jacket.

There was a commotion going on in Nev's office. He and the head stood together in animated conversation. Julia hadn't seen such a smile on Nev's face since the Ofsted inspector's last visit had ended.

'They're back,' he said. 'Every single file. We're saved!'

Julia rushed over to check. It was a mistake, she was convinced. Abbie had returned the other files, but hers wouldn't be there. But a swift glance through the piles showed that indeed they were.

'I'm going to put the lot of them under lock and key before they disappear again,' Nev said.

'I'll give you a hand,' Jim said.

Julia sat there, relief flooding through her. Just then Ed appeared at the door.

'I've just heard,' he said.

'Was this you?' she said, turning round at the sound of his voice. 'Did you get him to see sense?'

'I'd like to take the credit for it,' Ed said, 'but I never even got round to sending Jordan a text.'

'So who . . . ?'

Abbie and Seth came forward, standing together shyly. They looked very cosy, she couldn't help thinking. Were they holding hands?

'Perhaps we should go and get a pizza or something,' Ed said. 'There's a lot to explain.' He turned to the two teenagers. 'Do you fancy that?'

Abbie and Seth exchanged glances. Julia saw immediately that sharing a pizza with a couple of old fogies wasn't remotely on their agenda.

And to be honest, as much as she was grateful for their contribution, which she was certain Ed was just as capable of explaining as they were, she wasn't sure if sharing a pizza with a couple of love-sick teenagers was her idea of a good time, either.

And from the relief on Seth's face when they said they had other plans, it was clear he felt exactly the same way.

Running

1

Paula was making herself a mug of tea when Mick, back from work, walked in on her. From the set of her shoulders and the fact that she didn't even bother to look up from her task to acknowledge him, it was obvious she still wasn't speaking to him.

The sound of canned laughter from the TV in the living room failed to make so much as a tiny tear in the heavy cloak of resentful silence Paula had tightly wrapped around herself. As it scraped the sides of the mug, the repetitive clink of the teaspoon added to the mood of reproach that filled the kitchen.

Round and round it went. Clink, clink, clink. Some tea must have splashed over the sides because she tutted and reached over for a cloth to mop up the spillage. Paula liked things pristine. She thrived on order and routine. That was partly what the row last night had been about.

'I've been in touch with that Jody Martin.'

That was how it had started. With one short statement of fact. But Paula saw it as something else. The first step to the dismantling of her ordered world. And last night she'd made her feelings about the short phone call he'd made to the witness protection officer very clear.

They'd had a nice evening up to then. It could almost have passed for a 'before' evening. Over their meal, they'd all exchanged news about their day. Mick told them about one of the cabbies who'd delivered a baby in his cab.

Paula chipped in with a snippet about Julie, her younger sister, who she suspected had her eye on one of the blokes at work because, when she'd popped in on her way back to collect their mother's ironing, she'd been dressed up to the nines, full slap, stilettos, the lot. Mick had replied that he wished her luck, but he wished the poor chap she was after even more luck, and they'd had a bit of a giggle about that.

Then Leanne went on to announce

she'd got another A for her History essay, and that her teacher had said that if she kept it up she was definitely on course for a starred A in her GCSE exam the following year. Never one to be outdone, Andrew announced he had been chosen to be the narrator in his class assembly.

What had they done to deserve such clever children? Mick had said then. He winked at Paula, who'd smiled lovingly at all of them and said how very proud she was of both her kids. Then she'd asked who wanted ice cream. Last night, they'd put the Waltons to shame.

After the meal had been cleared away, the kids had drifted off to their rooms as usual. And that's when he'd broached the subject of the appointment he'd made.

'But why? I thought we'd agreed we didn't need any witness protection scheme.'

Paula always went from nought to 90 on the fury scale in a matter of seconds. Tonight was no exception. There'd been one small window of opportunity when he could have opened up to her and explained how he really felt, but she slammed it shut before he could muster up his courage. She reminded him exactly how he'd reacted when Jody Martin had talked to them the first time, just before the trial where Mick had given the evidence that had sent Euan Ferguson to prison.

Not that Mick needed reminding. Jody Martin had told them she thought they ought to know that this was not the first time Euan Ferguson had been before a court of law. She'd far sooner they learned the facts from her than discover some half-truths from the press, who would be bound to publish the information once the trial came to an end.

At his previous trial, Ferguson had been cleared of attempted murder, even though everyone knew he was as guilty as sin. They just hadn't been able to make it stick. According to Jody, a key witness had stood down at the last minute and, although he'd refused to say why, the reason had been pretty clear to everyone involved. He'd been intimidated by someone on the outside linked to Ferguson, who himself was being held in custody. Had the witness found the courage to go through with giving his evidence, Jody said, Ferguson would definitely have been sent down for ten years at least.

The police were desperate for Mick to go ahead and give his evidence, she said. After all, he was one of their key witnesses. But her loyalty didn't lie with the police or the courts but with witnesses who felt intimidated. That was what the witness protection scheme was for. Mick only had to say the word and she would be able to set in motion a chain of events that would get the family right out of the neighbourhood — to the other end of the country, if need be. In no time, the children could be settled into new schools and Mick and Paula into new jobs.

Even now, more than a month after the trial, Mick couldn't have explained to himself why he'd reacted the way he had. Was it an age-old macho instinct of never showing weakness in front of women, and in front of Paula in particular? Or was it just one more manifestation of how he usually coped with any information he didn't like the sound of? By opening his mouth and reacting immediately before he engaged his brain?

If he'd only paid closer attention to what Jody Martin had told him, he'd have realised that she was on his side. It hadn't been her intention to suggest that he was a wimp who couldn't take the stress of standing up in court and saying what he'd seen that morning, when he'd been unlucky enough to be driving down the stretch of road where Euan Ferguson, seized by road rage, had attacked and killed the poor driver who'd been driving the car behind.

But Mick had never been that good at paying attention. Paying attention meant shutting up and listening and carefully processing everything you'd been told.

He'd been full of bravado, bragging that he wasn't frightened of giving evidence in open court. Ferguson was a villain, and if Mick's evidence could put him away, then he'd leave court with his head held high.

Besides, he was a father of two children, he reminded her, and he wanted them to be proud of him. What kind of an example would he be setting them if he bottled out at this stage?

Even as the words left his mouth, he couldn't help thinking how pompous he must sound. But if Jody Martin agreed with him, her face didn't betray it. She simply nodded and smiled affably.

'Your sentiments are admirable, Mick,' she said. 'And I wish more people were as willing to come forward as you clearly are in order to help the law put away a villain. Believe me, it's not my intention to frighten witnesses into the scheme. But we do have to ask because some witnesses are too afraid to speak up for themselves.'

He must have infected Paula with his he-man display because that's when she piped up. 'Well, Mick's not,' she said, glaring at Jody Martin to bring home the point.

Paula went on to say quite a bit more, too. About how she had family here — her elderly mother, who relied on her to do her washing and shopping. Then there were her brother and sister and their families, not to mention friends and neighbours they'd grown up with all their lives. There was the kids' schooling to be taken into consideration, too. In short, upping sticks to the other end of the country was unthinkable.

'This is our home,' she said indignantly. 'We don't know anywhere else.'

Mick had nodded vigorously as Paula made the case for staying put. Yet already he was beginning to feel uneasy. While Paula had been holding the floor, there'd been time for Jody Martin's words to sink it.

The thought that Ferguson might actually be capable of getting back at Mick suddenly struck him as being a distinct possibility. But after everything he'd just come out with, he couldn't say he'd changed his mind without looking a complete fool in front of both women.

'We'll get through it,' he said. 'We're the Ashworth family and we won't be intimidated.'

A professional smile had flickered over Jody Martin's face then. She held out her card, told him to ring her any time if he had any more questions or if he suddenly found he wasn't managing very well. Paula, quick as a flash, tried to intercept it, but Jody Martin dodged her and made sure it went into the hand she'd intended it for.

'Listen to my husband. We'll manage very well, thank you,' Paula said, miffed at the snub.

'I'm sure you will,' Jody said, perfectly politely.

Three days later, after other witnesses had come forward to give evidence, after countless examinations and cross-examinations, after the jury had retired and deliberated before eventually returning with its verdict, Ferguson was put away for 20 years for the brutal murder of Lee Parr.

And Mick suddenly found he couldn't sleep. Night after night, he tossed and turned. When he did drop off, he was immediately startled awake again, as the scene he'd glimpsed so briefly, but for long enough to allow it to imprint itself on his memory, replayed over and over.

He heard the screech of car brakes; saw Ferguson leap out of his car and drag the other man out of the car he was driving;

91

saw too the raised arm and the glint of the knife in the morning sunlight. It was all over in seconds. Through his rear-view mirror, he glimpsed the victim raise his arms in self-defence before crumpling and falling to the ground, unable to believe the truth of his own eyes till much later, when he'd heard the man was dead, on the police appeal for witnesses.

Mick hadn't gone to court to hear the verdict. He'd heard it later when he turned on the TV to hear the news. He heard, too, how Ferguson's face had registered no emotion as the judge read him his sentence, and how his mother had broken down in loud sobs before being led away.

Now it wasn't just the memory of the incident itself that played on Mick's mind and kept him awake at night, but also Ferguson's apparent lack of remorse for what he'd done. It was obvious the man was pure evil.

These days, the slightest upset filled him with anxiety. He worried if the kids were even a minute later home from school than they usually were. He worried if Paula failed to answer her phone when he rang her and, more and more, he began to conjure up a scene in which he drove somewhere to pick up a fare, only to find that it was be some mate of Ferguson sent to get revenge. It was after he'd been through this scenario half a dozen times or more that he rang Jody Martin and made an appointment to speak to her.

But last night when he'd told Paula of his intentions to go and see Jody Martin at the end of the week, she'd gone berserk.

'What? About the witness protection scheme?'

Already he could see her brain ticking over, drawing conclusions, putting forward objections. It was only a meeting, he said. To find out what it actually entailed.

'Why didn't you discuss it with me first?' she said. 'We always discuss things jointly.'

He had no excuse, but he made one. It was a spur-of-the-moment thing. He couldn't see what harm it would do.

She was picking at a mark on the cooker with her thumbnail. Pick, pick,

pick. What she said next was devastating.

'You never should have come forward in the first place when the police were calling for witnesses.'

She raised her eyes from the hob and glared at him. It was like she hated him. With that look, Mick felt himself shrivel up inside. So. That was it. That's what she truly felt. That was the opinion she'd been holding back all these months. Never mind about doing the right thing. Getting justice for a dead man and putting a vicious murderer away.

Euan Ferguson had been banged up, thanks to Mick's evidence as much as anything else. It was something to be proud of, wasn't it? When he asked Paula the question, she didn't answer. Just went back to picking at that spot on the cooker. He felt like he'd let his family down.

The silence between them had started from that moment. Paula could keep it up indefinitely. He, on the other hand, wanted it sorted. He'd never been able to endure her moods.

Now, in the kitchen, with the humourless canned laughter in the background, it seemed she'd finished stirring her tea at last. Picking up her mug, she pushed past him to get to the door.

'I'm going for a lie-down,' she said. 'If my mother rings, tell her I'll be round tomorrow.'

Her eyes flickered over his face, registering disappointment and contempt. There was a second just before she averted her eyes when he could have told her the truth. That, actually, he was scared and no longer felt safe in his own home. And he didn't know for how much longer he would be able to keep up this game he was playing with the whole family that he was Superman. But the moment had already passed. Paula was already closing the door behind her.

★ ★ ★

In her office, Jody Martin was finishing typing up her notes before she left. She liked Mick Ashworth. The first time they'd met, she'd thought him a bit cocky. And a touch pompous, admittedly. But she'd been wrong. He'd been playing a role, that was all. Inside her office, without the wife in tow, he'd let his guard down. They'd had a row, Mick said. Paula hadn't spoken to him for days. She'd accused him of going behind her back by coming here. But it wasn't like that at all, he said.

'I've been having these nightmares. When I sleep, that is. The truth is — well, I'm not managing very well.'

Jody's expression of sympathy was genuine. He looked drawn, like a man with a lot on his mind. How long had it been since the trial? she'd asked him conversationally. It would get easier with time.

'No,' he said. 'You're wrong. It's getting worse. I keep thinking Ferguson's coming to get me. And I can't tell Paula how I feel. I have to protect her, don't you see? It's what I've always done.'

It wasn't Jody's place to judge. But sometimes it was hard not to. She thought she understood this marriage. Mick got his dinner on the table every night and a clean shirt every morning; Paula got someone to pay the bills and put the bins out.

The perfect compromise. Wedded bliss. She'd never been a fan.

'Paula didn't seem unduly disturbed that Ferguson might in some way be a threat to you and your family the last time we spoke.'

'You're right. But she was taking her lead from me, can't you see?' he said. 'I couldn't let her see that I was bothered by what you said.'

Men! What were they like?

'Are you asking to go on the witness protection scheme, Mick? Is that why you're here?'

He stared at his hands. She was never going to get him to admit that he was unless she dragged it out of him, and she wasn't going to be accused of coercing him. If she did move the family and it turned out badly for them, she didn't want to be blamed for it 12 months down the line. In circumstances such as these, she'd always found it best to keep out of it and stick to the facts.

'If you do agree to it, you're going to have to move right away from the neighbourhood, Mick,' she said. 'You leave with very little notice and with one suitcase between you, and you don't come back. And you tell no one where you're going. In fact, you won't know where you're going till you get there.'

'But what about our family?' Mick was visibly shocked. 'Surely we can let them know where we are?'

She shook her head. 'No, Mick. You must have nothing to do with them. No phone calls, no texts, no social networking sites. As far as your extended family and your friends are concerned, you've upped sticks and gone.'

Mick leaned back in his chair, clearly discomfited.

'I don't know,' he said. 'If it were just me . . . '

Perhaps he should go home and be as honest with Paula as he'd been with her, Jody said. Tell her how he really felt. That he didn't think he was capable of protecting her any more and he'd feel safer if they moved.

'I can't,' he said. 'Paula's family is everything to her. And then there's the house.'

It was a little palace, apparently, which

was an alien concept to Jody, who didn't care where she lived as long as there was a decent takeaway around the corner. But then she'd never been attached to bricks and mortar. In fact, she'd go as far as to say that she felt the same way about property as she did about marriage. And as for family . . . Well, she wasn't even going to go there. Best thing she'd ever done was leave home at the age of 18 and visit as infrequently as was still deemed polite.

In the end, the meeting with Mick had been inconclusive. To misquote the words of the song, 'He wouldn't say no and he wouldn't say yes'. And he wouldn't take her advice about going home and patching it up with Paula, either, so that they could sit down together like the adults they were meant to be and discuss their options.

'OK, then,' she said to the empty room as she switched off her computer for the day. 'Ball's in your court, Mick. I'm going home.'

Which was always the moment for her phone to start ringing. It was Terry

Greenhalgh, the DI who'd gone after Ferguson and put him away. One of the few people who had her number, given the nature of her job, where she could quickly become a criminal target if it ever got into the wrong hands.

'Terry, to what do I owe the pleasure?' she said cheerfully.

'I don't think you'll be very pleased when you hear my news,' he said.

* * *

Paula had had her nap. Now she was serving up their evening meal, her mouth a thin line of determination that she was not going to be the one to answer the phone. Mick dragged himself out of his armchair to do the honours. It was Jody Martin.

'Have you spoken to Paula yet, Mick?' She sounded much more brusque than he'd remembered her.

'I haven't had a chance yet.'

He didn't say it was because she'd barely acknowledged him since he'd arrived home.

'I'm not going to beat about the bush, Mick,' Jody said. 'But you've got a decision to make.'

'How — what do you mean?'

'I've just had a call from DI Terry Greenhalgh. He's got some bad news. They've found a body. Shot in the head in his car in a multi-storey a couple of miles away. One of the witnesses in Euan Ferguson's trial.'

Mick's heart suddenly started thumping. He was sweating and his breath came in short gasps. He needed to sit down.

'We're here for you, Mick. We can move you. The whole family. You only have to say the word.'

What was he supposed to do now?

'Ring me back in 15 minutes,' she said. 'If you say yes, then you've got two hours to pack.'

2

Six weeks had passed and now they were on the move again.

'Why?' a puzzled Andrew wanted to know. 'We've only just got here.'

'We're going back home, aren't we? That's why we're moving.' Leanne's face lit up expectantly.

She was such a pretty girl when she smiled. But smiles from Leanne were rare these days; ever since the move, she'd swapped them for a mask of snooty indifference. It flashed through Paula's mind that the expression on her daughter's face was a replica of what Mick must see on her own face these days. Mick should have been here now, explaining why they had to move again. But he'd gone off somewhere in a strop, thanks to that witness-protection officer.

Leanne began to do a little dance on the spot. 'I'm right, aren't I? Tell me I'm right!'

'I'm afraid not, love,' Paula said.

Leanne's face fell.

'We can't go home, Leanne, remember?'

She'd said it so many times now, yet neither of them seemed to have taken it in. Youth wasn't wasted on the young, whatever anybody said. Only young people could be so stubbornly optimistic, so sure that bad news could turn back into good, merely because they willed it so.

'This place was only ever temporary, remember? Now we have to move to the permanent place they've — your dad's — found for us.'

She tried to catch Leanne's eye to warn her to watch her tongue in front of her little brother, but Leanne pretended not to notice.

Mick and Paula had agreed on very little recently. But one thing they did decide was that, although it was going to be impossible to keep anything from Leanne, Andrew had to be protected from the truth.

He was still a child. For him, good still

triumphed over evil. If he found out there was someone out there who'd succeeded in killing one witness on behalf of another murderer in the spirit of twisted revenge, and who was fully prepared to pursue Andrew's own father, too, then it would destroy his trust in truth, goodness and justice for ever.

As far as he was concerned, the family was moving because Dad had a new job which he couldn't start until his references had been cleared — a flimsy story but one that Andrew, who'd never been one to show much curiosity, had swallowed. Meanwhile, they'd be staying in this holiday cottage until the new house was ready.

A barrage of questions — resentful on Leanne's part, excited on Andrew's — followed Paula's news. She attempted to answer as equably as possible, though it was a struggle to keep her own resentment at this latest turn of events out of her voice.

No, she wasn't sure exactly when they'd be leaving, but if it was anything like last time, they wouldn't be given much notice, so it might be a good idea to have an emergency case packed. Yes, the new house was bound to be bigger than this place, so that was something to look forward to, wasn't it? And finally, the answer to the question that was most important to them: definitely, they'd be going to school at last, instead of having to share a one-size-fits-all tutor.

'You'll both be pleased about that, won't you?' she added hopefully. 'You can make new friends at last.'

'I don't want new friends,' Leanne snapped. 'I want the friends I left behind.'

'I know you do, sweetheart,' Paula said.

Leanne and herself had so much in common, if only Leanne knew. Paula missed her friends, too, and missed her mother and her sister, Julie, and brother, Liam, all the time. Their absence in her life was a deep ache that never went away. She thanked God that Julie and Liam were there to take their turn in looking after Mum.

But no one was ever going to be able to accuse her of being disloyal. She'd married Mick for better for worse.

Perhaps they'd had their better and now they were stuck with their worse. Far easier to keep busy and at least maintain some sort of civility towards Mick so that the children wouldn't pick up any discord.

Which was exactly what she'd resolved to do when she'd woken up on the first morning after their arrival here. She'd simply put her emotions out of sight like a pile of unsightly rubbish you shoved away in a drawer before visitors called. But that drawer had proved to be far too flimsy to contain them. They'd developed this annoying habit of worming their way out when, as now, she was feeling at her most vulnerable.

'Come and give me a cuddle,' she said to Leanne, even though she knew she was wasting her breath.

'I'm going to pack my personal belongings,' Leanne said gruffly, making it clear that the suggestion was repulsive to her. 'I'm not having strangers rummaging around in my private things like last time.'

'Good idea, love.' Paula spoke the

words mechanically to her daughter's retreating back.

Immediately, Andrew was in her arms, hugging her tight as if sensing her sadness.

'Will they have computers at this new school, Mum?' He looked up at her, his huge eyes shining with excitement.

'I expect so, my love,' she said.

Where they were staying now, there was no internet connection and, after Jody Martin had warned them to be on their guard against the children using social-networking sites to contact old school friends, she and Mick had been glad of it.

The kids had gone berserk during that first two or three weeks of internet deprivation, Leanne more than her brother. There had been one hell of a row when they'd taken away her mobile, too, at Jody Martin's suggestion. Recently, however, they seemed to have got used to being without both phone and internet, only mentioning it occasionally, like today.

'I'm going to do some packing, too,' Andrew said, suddenly pulling away from her embrace. 'I want to make sure I've got my comic to read on the journey.'

Reluctantly, Paula let him go and wandered off into the kitchen to look for something to do. But, of course, there was nothing to do. She'd completed all the chores hours ago and, since she had neither friends nor family here, and because her husband seemed to prefer his own company to hers these days, she'd drawn a blank underneath the rest of the day. This wasn't life, she decided, reaching for the kettle; it was limbo.

* * *

Finally, Jody's breathing had steadied itself and the tightness in her chest was beginning to ease. Just as she always did after a long run, she went straight into her stretches. Oh, the relief! That was so good! This was the part she enjoyed most — another opportunity to revel in the fact that she'd managed to complete the distance one more time.

For the first time, she opened her eyes and focused on the view. Some people didn't think much of the scenery around here. DI Terry Greenhalgh, for one. Boring and flat, was how he described it once, when she happened to find herself on one of her visits to the police station.

She'd thrown her bag down on a nearby desk and her running shoes had fallen out. He'd asked her what she was in training for and she'd said 'Life', which made him crack his face. Terry Greenhalgh was far too cool to smile like normal people did.

Then he'd made his comment about the lack of good views around these parts. Where he came from — somewhere near Manchester she guessed from his accent — they were surrounded by hills. Now there was a challenge, he said, puffing out his chest like he'd personally made some significant contribution to those hills being there in the first place.

Jody had made no attempt to explain what the flatlands had to offer. She could have said how awestruck it made her feel to be standing in the middle of so much unbroken space and how easy it was to believe it was possible to fall off the world's end, like people used to do. Instead, she'd simply shoved her shoes back into her bag and excused herself.

The wind was getting up now, and dark clouds were beginning to roll in. She ought to get back. She had work to do. Since this morning, when she'd made that phone call to the Ashworths to tell them they'd soon be moving again, she hadn't been able to stop thinking about them. It was hard not to put herself in their place. Her mind drifted back to the training course she'd attended as a new witness-support officer.

'I want you all individually to name something in your life you'd hate to be separated from,' the course leader, Avril, had started by saying.

Without exception, everyone said they'd miss people the most. When it was Jody's turn, she was stuck for words. She'd always been a bit of a loner, and generally referred to people in her life as acquaintances rather than friends. She'd moved around a lot, too, and was used to leaving people behind, always promising — and failing — to stay in touch. When it was her turn to speak, she braced herself and went for the truth.

'I go running,' she said. 'Last year, I got injured. I couldn't run for a month. It was torture. I felt like killing myself.'

'So you'll understand how it must feel to someone on the witness-protection scheme to be wrenched from home, the place they love best, forbidden to explain why they're leaving and where they're going and with no time to say their goodbyes.'

In that moment, she'd understood exactly how it must have felt.

The sharp crack of a breaking twig jolted Jody back to the present. She spun around just in time to glimpse a squirrel scampering up a nearby tree. Immediately, she relaxed.

In her job, it was hard not to be permanently on her guard. She was aware that her knowledge of the new addresses of vulnerable witnesses made her just as vulnerable as they were. She often wondered if running alone, miles from anywhere and sometimes in the dark, too, was a risk too many. But, like she'd told Avril, she could never even think of giving it up.

He would show them — Paula, Jody
Martin and anyone else who tried to palm
him off with a job he didn't want. He was
a cabbie. Had been for 15 years. Maps
had always been his thing. He knew how
to find his way about.

That's what he'd been doing ever since
they'd been scooped up with no notice
like a handful of loose change and flung
down in this town he'd never heard of
before, where he knew no one and
everyone spoke in an accent that he
struggled to understand. Walking. Finding
short cuts. Killing time by learning the
Knowledge, as cabbies everywhere called
it. He was a quick learner. He could do it.
He *would* do it!

This morning, when Jody Martin had
rung to tell them they were on the move
again, her optimism — at least, until
she'd dropped this bombshell — had
been infectious.

He couldn't help admiring her way of
looking at life, envying it enough to try to
emulate it, too. There was no such thing

as catastrophe, she maintained — only setbacks and rough patches. After what she'd just told him, however, he'd gone right off her. She was just spinning him a yarn.

He was almost inclined to agree with Paula, for once. All right for her to carry on like Pollyanna, she'd maintained. Nobody's turfed her out of her home and separated her from *her* family.

Every time he thought of Paula nowadays, he felt depressed. She'd changed so much. What was done was done and now it was time to look forward. Surely, even if it was just for the sake of the kids, she should be able to see that.

They used to pull together all the time. They were a team. But since they'd moved, it was like she'd closed down and was just going through the motions of a marriage.

All he ever got from her these days was that look of scorn and disappointment. She made him feel like a waste of space. It was obvious to him she'd made up her mind that she wasn't even going to bother trying to make a go of it. And if it was obvious to him, then it must have been obvious to the kids, too, which was the worst bit.

'You'll like it,' Jody had said of the next town they'd be moving to. 'It's got good schools, great amenities, and your new home's in a lovely neighbourhood.'

When it sank in that this time their move was permanent, Mick came out with the plan he'd secretly been hatching over the last six weeks. If she'd tell him the name of the town they were moving to, he could nip out and buy an *A To Z* and start learning it.

'What for, Mick?' Jody had wanted to know.

'So I can get myself a cabbie's job.' Mick was surprised she should even have needed to ask. 'That's what I do. Drive cabs.'

'But I've sorted you a job, Mick. Delivery driver. It's yours for the taking.'

He'd never been one to lose his temper. But something stirred inside him. The flame of frustration he'd been damping down all these weeks suddenly flared up, fanned by her words.

'White van man?' he snapped. 'No way. That's not what I do.'

He'd said a lot more, too, and to give her credit, Jody Martin had listened patiently to his outburst until it fizzled out, when he began to wonder if her silence was because she'd put the phone down. She hadn't. But she was still adamant that he had to take this job he didn't want.

'Maybe in a few months, Mick, you can think about cabbying,' she said. 'But it's a big town. Bigger than where you used to live. It'll take you months to crack the Knowledge. What will you live on while you're doing that? You know there's no more money once we've given you the wherewithal to start your new lives — the car and the stuff you need for the house, etc.'

She was talking to him the same way Paula talked to the kids when she was about to deny them something they thought was their God-given right to own. He reached out, clutching at a passing straw.

'Just tell me the name of the place

we're moving to,' he pleaded. 'I'll go out now and get an *A To Z*. I'll start learning it straight away.'

The pause at the other end of the line was a lengthy one. Finally, she spoke.

'Mick, you know I can't,' she said. 'I can't risk you saying something to somebody.'

'Who? I never speak to anybody except the newsagent,' he snapped.

'The kids, Mick. Or Paula. How many more times do you want to move? If it accidentally got out through one of them, we'd have to move you again, don't you see?'

He hadn't thought about that.

'Would you want to put the family through all that again?'

She was using blackmail now. Of course he wouldn't and she knew it. They'd never forgive him. Things were bad enough already. He was already *persona non grata*. Paula hated him, Leanne definitely hated him, and even Andrew looked at him funny these days, in a way that suggested the scales had fallen from his eyes and he'd sussed that his father wasn't Superman after all, but an ordinary bloke, and a disappointing one at that.

'I know it's hard at the moment, Mick.' Jody's voice was softer now. 'But trust me. It'll be fine. You just have to give it time.'

He wished he could believe her. But right now, it was hard to see a time when life could ever get back to how it was.

* * *

Ben Cooper's phone had come into Leanne's possession by accident, just two days before they'd had the order to leave the house. She'd had no idea initially who it belonged to when she glimpsed it sticking out from beneath the bathtub in her friend Sam's bathroom, where she'd gone to get away from the noise and the crush of the party. Sam's parents had been away, and a load of kids from her school had taken full advantage.

It was just, at first, a phone, carelessly dropped and ignored, until she bent down and picked it up. There, in the privacy of the loo, while muffled sounds of celebration and the insistent driving beat of the bass came creeping up the stairs, a curious Leanne scrolled down the contacts list, to see if she could identify the mobile's owner.

It didn't take Sherlock Holmes to work it out. She shouldn't have been surprised that it was his. Ben was well known for losing things — his homework in particular! When someone hammered on the door yelling to be let in before they threw up, she'd slipped it into her pocket, unsure as yet what she was going to do with it.

Back home, after the party, she lay in bed mentally enacting all the different scenarios she could imagine between herself and Ben when she returned his property. It was an opportunity too sweet to waste. She'd fancied him for ages. Unfortunately, he was going out with some girl from another school, which was a bit of a complication. But if she went about this the right way, who knew how it might end? It was with this thought that she finally fell asleep.

The following day was a Sunday and

there was an atmosphere in the house. She'd removed herself to her room to escape it, remembered the phone and taken it out, scrolling down to Ben's address book again. When she reached 'Home' she stopped. If only she had the nerve to call his landline.

But what would she do if Ben picked up? Over and over, she practised her words. 'Hello, Ben. It's Leanne. Have you missed your phone yet?' Would that do? she wondered. Did it hit the right casual note?

In the end, she bottled it, deciding to wait until the following day, a school day, where opportunities to return it would surely abound. And if they didn't, then she'd have to manufacture one. But then they got the message that they had two hours in which to pack, and the whole household was thrown into total disarray. Temporarily at least, she forgot all about it.

When Mum demanded she hand her mobile over almost as soon as they'd set foot over the threshold of the new place, she'd made a terrible scene. It was only afterwards, when she'd exhausted herself screaming and shouting and had stormed off to the bedroom she now shared with Andrew, to fling herself on the bed, that she remembered Ben's phone. All was not lost, after all. Ben would help her get back in touch with her friends. He would be her go-between. Who knew what it might lead to?

Leanne closed the bedroom door behind her, cursing the fact that she had to share it and couldn't lock her little brother out like she used to be able to. Hopefully, while he was downstairs cuddling Mummy like the big softie he was, he'd be out of the way for as long as this was going to take her.

After easing the mobile from its hiding place among her underclothes, she clambered into bed, pulling the covers up around her. Then, scrolling down to the contact list, she quickly found Ben's home number. Taking a deep breath, she pressed 'select'. There. Done. 'No going back,' she thought as, after a moment's silence, the ringing tone began.

When Ben answered, almost immediately, Leanne was glad she'd thought to lie down, because otherwise she might well have passed out with nerves. Only now did it occur to her that it could have been his mum who'd answered. What on earth would she have done then?

'Ben, it's Leanne,' she whispered. 'Don't say anything. I'm not allowed to talk to anyone from home. But I'll go crazy if I don't . . . '

3

'Leanne? Leanne Ashworth?'

Ben had taken some time to respond. How many Leannes did he know? she wondered.

'Yes,' she said. 'That's right.'

She felt awkward, like she was intruding on Ben's precious time. She'd expected him to fall over himself in his excitement at being the first to hear from her after such a long time. But there was not the slightest trace of curiosity in his voice. He could have been taking a call from a complete stranger.

'How did you get my number?'

'I found your phone. At Sam's. I was going to give it back to you. But then — well, something happened and I wasn't able to come back to school again.'

'Doesn't matter anyway. I got a new one now. It's great. Does loads of stuff.'

Leanne felt herself shrinking inside. This conversation was meant to be about her. Had no one missed her? Had anyone even noticed she wasn't there any more?

'How's Sam?' she said. 'I'd love to talk to her, but you don't have her number on this phone.'

'She's hanging out with Jessica Aldred these days.'

Jealousy coursed through Leanne's veins. She felt sick. Sam was her best friend. How could she have latched on to someone else so soon? And Jessica Aldred, of all people.

'Are you still going out with . . . ?'

'Laura? Nah. I'm seeing somebody else now.'

'Oh?'

'Sam, actually. In fact, I'm meant to be meeting her at the bus stop in two minutes, so . . . '

'Oh, right.'

'Is that it, then? Only . . . '

'You've got to go.'

'Yeah. Nice talking to you.'

'You, too.'

'Oh and, Leanne . . . '

She gripped the phone tightly, holding her breath in anticipation.

'Yes?'

'You can keep the phone. Like I said, I've got a better one now.'

'Right.'

'Do you want me to give Sam a message? Get her to ring you?'

'No. It's OK.'

'See you then, Leanne. Stay cool,' he said.

He didn't even wait for her to say goodbye.

★ ★ ★

Mick had gone off to his new job at the crack of dawn. He would be delivering bread, cakes and pies to a chain of small local shops from the huge bakery that served them all. Paula hadn't asked him when he'd be back and he hadn't volunteered the information — anyway, she'd know soon enough, when he walked back in through the door.

Last night, half-heartedly, she'd asked him if he wanted her to get up with him in the morning, but he'd turned down her offer, gruffly replying that he'd see to himself. He was still harbouring his grudge with Jody Martin who'd got him the job — a grudge that last night had spread to herself.

After they'd eaten their meal, and Leanne and Andrew had cleared the table, he'd got out his brand new *A-Z*. She knew what he was up to. He thought this job as a delivery man wasn't good enough for him and he was determined to get back in a cab. He was lucky to have a job these days when so many didn't, but, of course, he was far too stubborn to appreciate that.

She'd made a comment — something about how on earth did he think he'd find the time to get to know his way round a brand-new town the size of this when he'd be getting up for work at five and would be dead on his feet by the time he came home?

He'd slammed the book shut then and shoved it in a drawer, muttering something sarcastic that sounded like, 'Thanks for your support'. For the rest of the evening, he hid behind the newspaper while she stared at the telly, not taking anything in. That's when, in a rare fit of guilt, she'd made her offer of getting up to see him off.

This morning she had heard him get up but had pretended to be asleep. Not long after she heard the front door shut, she got up herself, not wanting to risk oversleeping and making the kids late on their first day at their new school. The two of them had gone off together, shunning all offers of help.

'This is Andrew's first day at big school, Mum,' Leanne had reminded her. 'If he turns up with his mum, he'll be bullied for the rest of his time there.'

She'd stood at the window and watched them until they were out of sight, Leanne in front and Andrew, head down, trailing behind. When she could no longer see them, she realised she was on her own for the first time since the day Mick had come home and told her he'd been to see Jody Martin to discuss going on the witness-protection scheme. In that short space of time, their lives had been turned upside down.

Paula found herself envying Mick and

the children, as she wandered around from room to room putting things to rights and half-heartedly unpacking the boxes she hadn't got round to unpacking before. At least they were somewhere else other than shut up here in this house, which Paula didn't think she'd ever be able to bring herself to call home. They would meet people, too — make friends, even. What chance did she have of getting to know anyone, when she was stuck here on her own?

She hadn't worked since Leanne was born, but she'd never missed it. Her days had always been full. If she wasn't doing her own chores, she was off down at her mother's seeing to hers, which always included errands to the town to pick up this or that. Mick used to say that she did too much for her mother. Julie and Liam were working, she'd say, making excuses for her brother and sister. So they were, Mick agreed, but Julie was single and Liam, who was bone idle in Mick's view, had a wife who did everything for him. Between the two of them, they could have helped a bit more, surely?

He was right, of course. They could have done more. But then, if they had, how would she have filled her days? How was she going to fill her days now, with no one dependent on her?

While she was upstairs making the beds, she thought she heard something come through the door. A flyer, probably, since no one knew their new address. She decided to ignore it. Busy with her chores, she forgot all about it until Mick, back from his first shift, handed her an envelope he said he'd picked up off the mat.

'It's addressed to both of us,' he said, removing his jacket and slinging it over a chair back. Perhaps now was not the time to pick him up on it, though, Paula decided. Things between them were tense enough.

The envelope was addressed to *The new neighbours*. Intrigued, Paula opened it. It contained an invitation to pop next door to number 43 to say hello to Carole and Frank on Friday night. The words *Would have knocked but didn't want to intrude, Carole*, were added as a postscript.

'We can't go,' Paula said, passing back the note for him to read for himself.

'Why ever not?' Mick said.

'You know why not. We'd be tripping ourselves up every time we opened our mouths. What if we give ourselves away?'

'We won't. You know what Jody Martin said. Keep things simple and you'll be fine.'

'So you want to go, then?' Paula read the note again.

'It'll do us good,' he said. 'Especially you. You're the one stuck here on your own every day while the kids are at school and I'm at work.'

'And how was work?' Not brilliant, she guessed, from the way he'd so far failed to mention it at all.

'It's a job,' he said gruffly. 'Now, is there any chance of a cup of tea?'

*   *   *

In the end, they all went round to the neighbours, apart from Leanne, who said she had a headache. Mick was all for jollying her out of it, but Paula told him to leave her be. He decided to take her advice. The last thing he wanted was Leanne and her long face pouring cold water on an occasion that had the potential to turn into a jolly one. Thank goodness his son wasn't prone to black moods. And even Paula had made an effort with her hair and make-up and a dress.

'You look nice,' he said, as they stood outside the front door to number 43 waiting for someone to open it.

'Thanks,' she said, sounding quite pleased about something for once.

Carole and Frank were in their 40s, local to the area and with solid roots, so Mick gathered from the way they spoke about their family. Every age group, from their elderly parents to nieces and nephews of toddler age, seemed to be represented in every corner of the town, although they had no children of their own, which was a disappointment. It would have been great if Andrew could have found a playmate or Leanne a new pal.

But they did have a cat who'd just had kittens. They could go and see her in a bit, when they'd all had a drink and a warm by the fire, Carole said, but they didn't want to make Queenie nervous by all crowding in on her at once.

'You have to be so careful with mother cats,' she said to Andrew.

Mick liked the way Carole included Andrew in the conversation. He couldn't say the same for Frank, however, who more or less ignored Andrew after the initial introductions. While Carole fussed around them, plying them with food and drink, it was Frank who kept up the conversation. For the most part, this consisted of him doing the talking while everyone else listened.

On the upside, his lack of curiosity, aided by Carole's obsession with making sure they all had a drink and something to eat, succeeded in taking the limelight right away from Mick's own family. But on the downside, he soon grew tired of Frank's monologue, whose subjects touched on his allotment, the lack of gardening prowess in the neighbours who were here before them and the brilliance of Carole's sister's girl, who was studying Law at Cambridge University.

Now Frank was describing how he and Carole had met. It was a long tale with many twists and turns. Paula was only pretending to be interested, that much was obvious, and Andrew wasn't even bothering. He kept looking towards the door, probably wondering when he could go and see the kittens.

'The first time Paula and I hooked up it was a disaster,' Mick said, seizing on the opportunity to butt in when Frank paused briefly to take a sip of his beer.

As soon as his dad launched into his tale, Andrew began to wish he were a million miles away. How many times had he and Leanne had to sit through this story? he asked himself, wishing she were here now to share his torture.

Dad left nothing out — it was all there. The bit where he saw Mum across a crowded room at some party and told his best friend that this was the girl he was going to marry. The bit about how he didn't see her for weeks afterwards until, one day, she got on his bus and they got talking, and how, before she knew it, Mum had agreed to meet him at some pub for a drink. But then she'd got the name of the pub mixed up with another one with a similar name and so, when he never turned up, she left, furious, and went back home.

At this point, whoever wasn't telling the tale — in this case, Mum — would butt in to remind everybody that these were the days before mobile phones. True to form, Mum — whose warning glance Dad had ignored at the start of his tale but who'd now clearly got into the spirit of things — piped up with this obvious info at the correct moment, provoking loud sympathetic responses from the neighbours.

'So, what happened then?' Carole wanted to know.

Andrew longed to say, 'Well, isn't it flaming obvious?' But, of course, he didn't dare. Mum would have killed him once she'd got him home. Besides, he'd just noticed something. They seemed to be sitting closer together than before, less stiff, more relaxed, occasionally even touching each other and locking eyes as between them they cobbled together the rest of the story — he said, she said, and then, and then. It had been an awful long time since Andrew had seen his mum and dad so comfortable with each other.

'Well, what a lovely story,' Carole said, when Dad had got to the end.

Mum and Dad both grinned self-consciously and looked at their feet. But they hadn't moved away from each other, Andrew noticed. If anything, they'd moved closer.

'Right, Andrew,' Carole added, getting to her feet determinedly. 'I promised you a look at those kittens, didn't I? Anyone else want a peep?'

'Perhaps later,' Mum said. 'Too many visitors might frighten them.'

Dad nodded in agreement. 'Off you go with Carole, son,' he said. 'You can tell us all about it when you get back.'

It was with a light heart that Andrew followed Carole out of the room.

* * *

Leanne was still smarting from her phone call with Ben. She was furious with Sam, too. The two of them had been best friends since Year Nine when they'd found themselves in the same maths set, and had been inseparable ever since, both in and out of school.

What short memories everybody had! She'd never been the most popular girl in the school, but she'd always had her share of friends. Maybe not as many as Sam, who seemed to attract people like moths to a flame. Yet, even if she'd never been in Sam's league, she'd never before believed herself to be totally forgettable.

But in less than six weeks, it was as if she'd never existed . . . and now she was at this new school, where once again the signs were all pointing to her blending into the background, along with the rest of the Forgettables.

When she'd first arrived in her form room on Monday, people had shown some initial interest in her. But it had quickly waned. Evidently she'd failed to come up to scratch in some way — not pretty enough or outrageous enough, probably. People were polite to her, but that was as far as it went. Everyone seemed to be either paired up or in a group, and they weren't looking for anyone else to join the close-knit little clique it had taken them five years to build up.

Last night, as she'd lain in bed trying to get to sleep, Leanne decided she was fed up with being ignored and that she was going to do something about it. Luckily, she had an ace up her sleeve and once the weekend was over she intended to play it. They'd soon sit up and take notice of Leanne Ashworth once Monday came round.

What the..? A fierce hammering on the front door finally penetrated Leanne's earphones. She slid off her bed and crossed the landing to Mum and Dad's bedroom. Their window looked out on to the front, so whoever it was could be seen from there.

Common sense argued that if this was a murderer coming to exact his revenge on the family on behalf of Euan Ferguson, he'd find a more subtle way of going about it. But as she peeped outside from behind the curtains, fear was already beginning to nibble away the edges of her confidence.

'Let me in! Leanne! Open the door!'

It was Andrew and he was clearly in a right old state. Leanne, wondering what on earth was the matter with him, flew down the stairs to the front door, hastily yanking it open.

'Andrew! What's going on?'

'Get out of my way,' her brother yelled, pushing past her. 'Just leave me alone, will you?'

Leanne watched open-mouthed as he tore up the stairs three at a time before wrenching open his bedroom door and slamming it behind him.

★   ★   ★

Queenie the cat had given birth in the wardrobe in the spare bedroom, so Carole had explained, as Andrew had followed her up the stairs. She was a slow walker, leaning on the banister with every step she took while keeping up a monologue about how she'd read it was dangerous to move mother cats away from the place they'd given birth, so they'd left her where she was and tried to make it as comfy as possible for her and her new brood.

'This way, Andrew,' she said, once they'd reached the landing. 'Mind how you go.'

Carole apologised for the heat in the room, but said it was for the kittens. Andrew hadn't even noticed. He was only interested in the kittens. There were four of them — one black, one black and white, one ginger and one that Carole described as tortoiseshell, though all the different vibrant shades that made up this particular furry bundle were far more eye-catching than any tortoise he'd ever seen.

'They're beautiful,' he said.

He'd already decided that if only he could have a kitten of his own he wouldn't ask for anything else for ages.

'Do you think your mum and dad will let you have one?' Carole could have read his thoughts. Immediately, she put her hand to her mouth. 'Oh dear. Now they'll accuse me of putting ideas in your head.' Her blue eyes gleamed mischievously.

'Don't worry,' Andrew said. 'They're already there.'

After a while, the kittens grew curious. One by one, they began to teeter towards their visitors on unsteady paws, gradually growing more confident.

'They like you, Andrew,' she said. From the one chair in the room she removed the pile of old newspapers she'd explained were for the cat litter tray and plonked herself down on it.

'The heat in here's killing me,' she said, wafting her face with her hand. 'Do you mind if I leave you up here so you can play with them on your own? You can come downstairs when you've had enough.'

Andrew, relieved she wasn't suggesting they should both leave, quickly agreed. As soon as she closed the door, he got down on the floor and started playing with a ball of string he found that Carole must have left, alternately dangling one end in the air, then trailing it along the ground while the kittens fell over themselves to catch it. Then he lay down again while they crawled all over him, pausing occasionally to knead his sweater with their feathery paws.

Several enjoyable minutes passed like

this before Andrew, remembering what Mum always said about not outstaying your welcome, wondered whether he ought to go back down and join the grown-ups.

He was about to hoist himself up from the floor when his eye was caught by the headlines on the front page of the newspaper that lay on top of the pile Carole had brought with her.

WITNESS FOUND DEAD IN CAR, it said. Witness. He'd heard that word so many times over the last few weeks. Dad had been a witness. When he saw the name *EUAN FERGUSON*, he read on, intrigued.

This was the name of the man whose trial Dad had been a witness in. Quickly he read the rest of the story, his blood running cold as gradually it sank in that this same witness found dead in his car had also been a witness at the trial of Ferguson, and the police suspected that Ferguson had given the order for the murder from prison.

Head spinning, he started to piece it all together — the sudden move with no time to pack properly; the move to the new school; instructions from Mum and Dad: 'Remember, we've moved with Dad's job, that's all anyone needs to know.' Raised voices that ceased when he walked into the room.

They'd lied to him. Told him a fairy story. They were on the run from a murderer and his family was the next target. Andrew leapt to his feet, nimbly avoiding the kittens, and lunged towards the door. He had only one thought in his head. He had to get out of here!

4

The sound of thundering feet closely followed by the front door opening then slamming shut startled everyone, cutting Frank off in the middle of a monologue about his bindweed, much to Mick's relief.

'Was that Andrew?' Paula couldn't imagine why he would leave so unceremoniously.

'I'll just nip upstairs. Make sure he's closed the bedroom door behind him.' Carole eased herself out of her chair. 'We don't want those kittens escaping.'

It flashed through Paula's mind that Andrew may have caused some damage up in the bedroom where the kittens were kept — accidentally kicked over a bowl of water or, even worse, the litter tray. Too afraid to admit to what he'd done, he'd simply fled. She ought to check it out, to be on the safe side.

'I'll come, too,' she said.

At first glance, everything looked to be in order, apart from the kittens, who were running riot all over the floor. Even as Paula scanned the room for signs of damage, she couldn't help but be drawn to their playful antics.

'Oh, aren't they just impossibly cute!' she exclaimed.

She shifted her gaze to the same pile of newspapers that had caught Andrew's attention just a few minutes earlier. It took less than a second for the name of Euan Ferguson to leap out at her from the front page of the topmost one. Heart pumping fit to burst, she struggled to retain her composure. The last thing she needed was to arouse Carole's suspicion.

'I'm so sorry about Andrew,' she said. 'I can't think what got into him.'

'I expect someone rang him with a more exciting offer.'

Paula's gratitude to Carole for providing Andrew with an alibi was boundless. She wasn't to know he didn't have a phone.

'Yes,' she said. 'That'll be it. Still, I think we ought to go home now and have a word. Rushing off like that was bad manners.'

Carole brushed her words aside. 'Don't be too hard on him,' she said. 'He's a lovely boy. A credit to you both.'

Her words touched a tender nerve. Paula liked Carole. 'In other circumstances, we could be friends,' she thought. But if she could never be truly open then what sort of a friendship could it really be?

* * *

'Thank God you're back! Andrew's barricaded himself into his room.' Leanne looked at her wits' end. 'He won't say what's the matter. Just keeps telling me to go away.'

'He knows,' Mick said grimly.

'Oh.' The expression on Leanne's face was proof enough that she understood exactly what Andrew knew.

'I'll go to him.'

Without removing her coat, Paula dashed up the stairs. Leanne's eyes followed her anxiously.

144

'How did he find out?' she said, spinning round to face Mick.

Briefly, he explained. Leanne's reaction was not the one he expected.

'Good,' she said. 'I'm glad. We can all stop playing games now.'

Had he heard right? Mick's head was throbbing after too many beers. He badly needed a drink of water.

'He's just a child, Leanne,' he said. 'He shouldn't have to deal with this. It's too much for him.'

'It's too much for me, too! Have you thought about that?' Leanne suddenly burst into noisy sobs. 'No, you haven't. You never think about me. Either of you!'

Mick was lost for words. He needed Paula to come downstairs and take control. She knew how to deal with Leanne when she got emotional. But Paula had her hands full with this other drama. Mick made a clumsy attempt to take Leanne in his arms, scrabbling around to find the right phrase that would make things better.

'It'll be all right,' he said feebly.

'No it won't!' She pushed him away

with such force that he stumbled. Where on earth did all that strength come from?

'My life's over. My friends have forgotten all about me and neither of you could give a damn about me. It's only ever been about Andrew!'

'Leanne! No. You're wrong.' He wanted to say more. About how she was his pride and joy, but Leanne was in no mood to hear anything complimentary. Then Paula appeared at the top of the stairs, with Andrew, wheyfaced and tearful, at her side.

'Mick? Leanne? What's going on?'

'Chaos,' Mick wanted to say. 'Total, ruddy chaos.' If only he'd kept his mouth shut about what he'd witnessed. OK, so maybe his silence would have resulted in Euan Ferguson keeping his freedom. But it might have been worth it if it meant that he, too, could be free.

* * *

Paula didn't sleep much all weekend. Andrew had refused to leave her side for most of it, while Leanne, on the other hand, had kept to her room, only surfacing at mealtimes to sit in silence around the table before once more returning to her lair.

At least she and Mick made some headway with each other. When Paula told Mick how she'd explained things to their son — admitting that yes, a witness had been killed by someone acting on behalf of Euan Ferguson, but now the police had moved them this man would never find them — he reassured her that this was how he would have explained things, too.

And when Mick confessed how powerless he'd felt in the face of Leanne's fury, Paula said she made her feel just the same. Leanne was angry with them both, but what they had to remember was how tough it must be for her. Girls relied so much on their friends, she reminded him. It was understandable that she'd blame them for taking her away from them.

All they could do now was be patient with her and hope she made new ones. As for all this stuff about them favouring Andrew, well, that was just what siblings did. She'd been the same with her sister, Julie, when they were kids, she added.

Mick had brought up the subject of the trial then, launching into an apology for giving evidence. But Paula shushed him.

'I'm proud of you,' she said, realising that, actually, despite everything, she meant it.

She'd fallen in love with Mick because he was a good man. And she'd almost begun to hate him for the same reason. It made no sense, she saw that now.

When Monday morning dawned, Paula braced herself for another difficult week, but reminded herself that she'd resolved to be positive for the kids' sakes. She'd had an idea she hoped would go some way to alleviating the atmosphere in the house. Sitting with Mick, drinking a mug of tea while he got ready for work, she let him in on it.

'Your call, Paula,' Mick said, when she'd explained. 'You'll be the one doing all the work.'

'Well, you know me,' she said, with a rueful grin. 'I've always been a bit of a mug that way.'

'No, not a mug,' he said. 'A very caring person. I've just never given you proper credit for it before.' Mick rose from the table and planted a goodbye kiss on her cheek. 'Give Carole a ring later on,' he said.

'I will,' she said, feeling optimistic for the first time in a long while.

★ ★ ★

Her optimism lasted all of two hours. Then the children got up. Andrew was difficult from the moment he got out of bed, culminating in him declaring that he had no intention of going to school today or any other day.

Thankfully, Leanne didn't join her brother's mutiny. In fact, she seemed oddly keen to get going.

'Mum, tell him to get a move on,' she yelled from the door. 'I'm setting off in exactly five minutes.'

'Come on, Andrew. Play the game,' Paula pleaded lamely.

Already she knew in her heart of hearts that she'd lost the battle.

'No. I want to stay here where I'm safe,' he said. 'What if that man's found out where we live and he's waiting for us?'

'Don't be stupid, Andrew!' Leanne yelled.

'Ssh, Leanne. Don't speak to your brother like that.'

'Well, he is stupid,' she said. 'Stupid and annoying.'

Andrew launched himself at Leanne. She was ready for him and managed to fend him off easily.

'Enough!'

Paula laid her throbbing head in her hands. Squinting through her fingers, she winced at the sight of Leanne holding Andrew at bay. Her smirk of pleasure at her superior strength cut Paula to the quick. Never again would she pass judgment on badly behaved kids, she resolved. Not when her two had developed into monsters overnight.

'You go, Leanne. I'll bring Andrew in later.'

'I'm not going in at all, I said,' he insisted.

With one final contemptuous shove, Leanne let him go. Andrew slunk away towards the settee, where he threw himself down, curling himself up into a ball like a wounded animal.

'Spoiled brat. Mummy's boy.' Tired of baiting Andrew, she now turned her invective on to Paula. 'You never let *me* have a day off when I want one, do you?' she hissed.

'Leanne! Please.'

'Don't worry, I'm going.'

And then she was gone without so much as a goodbye. A lump formed in Paula's throat. It occurred to her that, if she never saw her daughter again, this ugly scene would be her final memory of her.

She would ring the Principal. He knew about their situation. He'd understand why Andrew couldn't make it today and why perhaps Leanne's behaviour might be a bit of a challenge for the staff.

★ ★ ★

During her first week at her new school, Leanne had had plenty of opportunity to stand on the sidelines and observe the hierarchy there. Last Friday afternoon, during double games, she'd sown her seed expertly.

With immaculate timing, she'd burst into tears in the girls' changing room at the exact same moment that Rebecca Jones, the most popular girl in Year 11, came out of one of the toilet cubicles.

Leanne knew how vital it was to her plan that Rebecca liked her. Since nobody liked a sniveller, she'd jumped up, dried her eyes and made to hurry off. Fortunately, as well as being clever and pretty, Rebecca Jones was also very kind and very curious about other people, traits that had no doubt earned her that popularity in the first place.

'It must be hard being the new girl,' she'd said sympathetically.

'It's not so bad,' Leanne replied. 'Under normal circumstances . . . ' But hers weren't normal circumstances. Naturally, Rebecca had been intrigued and longed to know more. When Leanne, stumbling over her words, whispered that she'd already said too much and scurried off, she'd set the scene for a display of interest in her this Monday morning, the like of which she'd never known before.

Of course, she only confided in Rebecca. And it had to be dragged out of her. That was at lunchtime when Rebecca insisted they went into the dining hall together.

'But what about your friends?' Leanne wanted to know.

'Never mind them,' Rebecca said. 'It's you I'm interested in. I want to know your story.'

That's when Leanne played her trump card. Her guarantee that, by the end of the day, everyone who was anyone would want to be her friend. Because nobody could possibly have a story half as interesting as hers.

'If I tell you, you must promise me you won't repeat anything I say to anyone else,' she insisted.

'Of course I promise,' said Rebecca, crossing her fingers behind her back.

★ ★ ★

Why wasn't Jody Martin, the Ashworths' witness-protection officer, picking up her phone? DI Terry Greenhalgh let out a string of expletives beneath his breath. 'You can always get me on my mobile' was the last thing she'd said when he'd told her they were this close to catching Euan Ferguson's scummy running dog and doing him for the murder of Jack Fisher, the other witness.

Things had moved on apace since this morning, when she'd breezed through the door like someone with a much more pressing agenda, leaving her words hanging on the air as she disappeared. What he had to tell her impacted on the Ashworth family.

Greg Kelly, Jack Fisher's murderer, had finally been arrested. It had taken a while and he hadn't come quietly, but then they rarely did. He was now sitting in a cell waiting for his brief, saying nothing.

It suddenly flashed through Terry's head where she might be. She'd been dressed for it, now he remembered, but he'd been far too keyed up about catching up with Greg Kelly to make the connection between her running shoes and her intentions until this instant. 'Call yourself a detective, Greenhalgh,' he muttered, heading for his car.

His phone rang. It was the governor of the prison where Ferguson was. He couldn't believe his ears when he heard the news. In fact, he made him say it twice just in case he'd misheard.

This was definitely his lucky day. Everything comes in threes, the saying went. Well, he'd had two good things happen to him already this morning. Jody Martin's face flashed into his head. Better not push his luck, he mused, as he switched on the ignition.

★ ★ ★

Paula was aware that the parenting manuals would probably frown on this. But if it took a kitten to get Andrew to promise to go to school, then a kitten it would have to be. Her bribery had worked. After lunch, he'd put on his uniform and walked with her as far as the school gate like a little angel, before trotting right up to the main entrance as if he was actually looking forward to going inside.

She glanced across at Mick, half dozing in the chair. These early mornings were killing him.

'Carole's going to bring the tortoiseshell one round after tea herself,' she said.

If only they could go back home. Last night, she'd dreamed about her mum, that she was poorly and was calling out for her. She'd woken up in a cold sweat and had been unable to get to sleep again.

When the phone rang, it woke Mick up. Snippets of Paula's one-sided conversation reached him through a fog of exhaustion. 'Yes, speaking. The Principal? You're ringing about Leanne?' And then a long pause. Or he may have drifted off again. More talking. 'Are you sure? How can it have got out? No. Yes. Of course you were right to inform me. Thanks.'

And then she was shaking him awake.

'Mick, we're in trouble.'

He blinked, not fully able to take in what she said at first. But very quickly it all became clear.

'We're going to have to ring Jody

Martin. Now,' he said, jumping up. 'If it's all round Leanne's school that we're on witness protection, how long will it be before some bright spark posts it up on the internet?'

'We're going to have to move again,' Paula said, bursting into tears.

★ ★ ★

Jody could have sworn there was someone following her. Running through the copse a couple of minutes back, she'd got the feeling she wasn't alone. Maybe she should have stopped, turned round and confronted her pursuer. But she was miles from anywhere, with no weapon.

Swerving away from her usual isolated route, she made a decision to head off instead towards the village. There would be people there. Safety in numbers. The sky was a mass of dark clouds and she felt raindrops on her cheek.

'Keep running,' she told herself. 'Don't be scared. No one knows where you are.' Euan Ferguson was locked up like all those other villains whose victims had turned to her for protection. But villains had friends who did their bidding. Even with all her checks, it was still possible that one day someone would come after her and force her to give up the new address of some witness, so that some terrible form of revenge could be exacted.

'Jody!'

She froze. Gathering all her strength, she upped her pace. She didn't see the rabbit hole until her foot was caught in it, sending her sprawling. No point struggling, she decided, as a long shadow fell over her.

'We've got him, Jody. Jack Fisher's murderer. And you'll never believe the best bit. Ferguson's dead. Heart attack.'

She looked up into the face of Terry Greenhalgh. He was grinning. The man who never smiled. Actually grinning.

★　★　★

'So Ferguson's really dead? And this Kelly's confessed to Jack Fisher's murder?'

When Jody Martin and a plain-clothes police officer appeared on his doorstep and asked if they could step inside, Mick had expected the worst. But it looked like he'd got it wrong.

'Tell me again what he said,' Paula said from her seat on the sofa next to him.

He was glad she'd asked, actually, since he'd taken very little in himself the first time. It had taken a good five minutes for his heart to stop knocking against his ribs and to start believing that Jody and this DI Greenhalgh weren't here to announce they were going to have to move again because of Leanne's loose tongue.

'He said he was no friend of Ferguson,' Jody Martin said. 'But that Ferguson had once got him out of a spot of bother. Unfortunately, when Ferguson got into a spot of bother of his own, he was required to repay the debt.'

'So he had nothing personal against Jack Fisher?' Mick said.

'That's right,' Jody replied.

'So that means he's got nothing personal against me, either.'

'Right again.' Jody beamed at him. 'You don't need to worry about either of them any more.'

Paula gripped the arm of the chair. 'Then we can go home, can't we?' She glanced from one to the other, breathing hard.

'Mrs Ashworth.' The Inspector cleared his throat and began to speak. 'The police owe a duty of care to witnesses at risk and . . .'

Mick didn't like the sound of this at all.

'For God's sake, Terry.' Jody glared at Greenhalgh. 'What he means, Mr and Mrs Ashworth, is that now your circumstances have changed, the level of risk has declined. There'll be a few formalities but yes, not tomorrow, probably not even for another month or two, but soon, you'll be able to return home and resume the lives you left behind.'

Relief flooded through Mick with all the power of a burst dam. Paula, by now sobbing joyfully, leaped up from her seat, launching herself first at Jody then at DI Greenhalgh, hugging them both. The final hug she reserved for Mick himself.

'Mum! Dad! What's going on?'

Leanne and Andrew, attracted by the commotion, stood in the doorway, Andrew clutching the tortoiseshell kitten, his bribe for promising to go to school.

'It's over, kids,' Mick said. 'We're going home.'

Leanne gave a loud whoop and hurled herself at Mick, who lifted her off her feet and swung her around. Paula was crying and laughing at the same time and so was Jody. Even the DI looked a bit damp around the eyes, Mick thought. Only Andrew remained unmoved.

'What's up, son?' Mick said.

Andrew stood there, hugging the kitten, his expression mournful.

'Does that mean I have to give Puddles back?' he said.

'Puddles?' Mick furrowed his brow. 'Daft name for a cat.'

But when he went into the kitchen to see if there was anything more celebratory to drink than tea and saw the state of the floor, he decided it wasn't a daft name at all. Ah, well, he sighed, as he cleared it up. They just had to hope that Puddles would be house-trained before moving day. And that was a day that couldn't come a moment too soon.

Beloved

1

Helen had been stuck in front of her computer for two hours now, trying to write her essay, and she'd had enough. What on earth had made her imagine she could take up her education again at the age of 40 la-la, when she'd been so rubbish at school first time round?

She used to tell the kids when they were younger, and still living at home, that fresh air helped if ever they got stuck with their homework. Perhaps a stroll to the library to return her biology textbook would help unstick her brain.

If Mandy and Jack were here now, she knew they'd return the encouragement. But Mandy was working as a beautician on board a cruise liner and Jack was even further away, in Australia. 'You're on your own, mate,' she told herself, grabbing her book, her bag and her jacket, and letting herself out of the house that, these days, was so eerily quiet.

As she made her way down the street, she reminded herself that, actually, she was much better off on her own than being stuck in a dead marriage. Her ex-husband had never encouraged ambition in her — maybe because he'd never had any himself. 'What on earth do you want with a degree?' she could imagine him saying.

'Because once upon a time, before I met you, Craig Walker, my ambition was to be a nurse,' she said softly, turning on to the main road. 'And now the kids have left and I'm on my own, I've got back that ambition.'

Of course, the down side to living alone was the habit she'd got into of talking to herself. She was in the middle of this thought when the deafening sound of a car horn and the screech of skidding wheels stopped her in her tracks.

The car had already disappeared before she'd had time to piece together what had happened and she spun around to see a figure in the middle of the zebra crossing struggling to get up off the ground. A man's shoe squatted forlornly next to him, and the contents of a plastic bag were scattered everywhere. Helen ran over to join the little group of people who'd run to his aid.

By now, the victim, a tall, well-built man around her own age, had managed to struggle to his feet and limp back to the pavement. In a strong foreign accent but otherwise perfect English, he repeatedly insisted he was fine. All he needed was a bit of help to pick up any shopping that was recoverable.

Obligingly, one of the passers-by who'd hurried over to help — a female jogger — ran into the road to retrieve what items she could. The pallor of the man's complexion, in stark contrast to his dark hair and brows, belied his insistence that he was fine. Helen knew she wouldn't be able to walk away as casually as the others were beginning to do until she could be certain he really was OK.

'How about a cup of tea?' she said when everyone had left. 'There's a café just down the bottom of this road. Let me buy you one.'

'Oh, no,' he said. 'Really, I don't want

to be any trouble.'

'I insist,' she said. 'You've had a shock. Come on.'

He smiled for the first time — a smile that couldn't hide his relief.

'In that case,' he said, 'it would be bad manners to refuse.'

It was just a stupid accident, he said as, 10 minutes later, they sat drinking their tea. He'd assumed the driver was going to stop, so had started to cross the road. When the car's wing mirror clipped him, he lost his balance and fell. That would teach him not to believe everything he'd read about England before he came to live here!

'I thought motorists were supposed to give priority to pedestrians at crossings here,' he said.

Helen agreed. 'They aren't supposed to leave the scene of an accident, either. Pity he'd gone before anyone got his car registration. Are you sure you're quite all right?'

'I'm feeling much better, thank you. I'm Stefan, by the way.'

'And I'm Helen,' she replied.

By the time they were on their second cup of tea, Helen had learned that Stefan had arrived in London from Lithuania less than six months ago to work in his cousin's business. The cousin lived in south London and he was staying with him until he found somewhere of his own. When she said it must be nice for him to have family here, he pulled a face. They didn't get on, he said. All his cousin was interested in was chasing girls and drinking beer. He wasn't interested in the culture that London had to offer or any of its history, either.

'I'd rather be in my own company than his,' he said, adding that he'd made a resolution to become as familiar with the streets of London as he was with those of Vilnius. He'd got into the habit of going out walking every weekend for hours at a time accompanied only by his *A-Z* and his guidebooks, to see what was to see.

'Is that what you were doing this morning?' she asked him. 'Discovering north London for the first time?'

He was about to reply when her mobile rang. It was her study buddy, Neil. They'd met at the start of the new term at college, the two oldest students by 20 years in some cases, and had drifted together during that first coffee break, perhaps in silent, instinctive acknowledgement that they were allies in a sea of youth.

When the tutor advised them to pair up with a classmate whom they could call in case they ever felt they needed to discuss a piece of work, Neil was the obvious choice.

During that first week of term, when everything had been new and frequently terrifying, Helen had rung or e-mailed Neil several times and he'd never been less than helpful.

As reluctant as she was to break off her conversation with Stefan, it was only fair she spoke to Neil. Thankfully, it was a brief exchange. His internet was down — could she check something for him online urgently? He wouldn't ask, only, unless he finished his essay within the next two hours, he wouldn't get the time before Monday to have another crack at it. When the call was over, she apologised to Stefan and told him she had to leave.

'Your husband must be wondering where you are,' he said.

'That was just a friend,' she said. 'I'm not married. Haven't been for many years.'

Later, when they'd parted and she was back home, she replayed that bit of the conversation in her head. Had it been her imagination, or had he looked pleased when she'd put him straight about her marital status? But, if that had been the case, wouldn't he have asked for her number? She'd been out of the mating game so long, she'd no idea of the rules any more.

★ ★ ★

The following Monday morning, there was a thick, padded envelope in her pigeon-hole. It contained the library book she'd been intending to return the day she'd met Stefan. All week, she'd fretted about its loss, even calling the café, where they'd said no one had handed it in. What a relief that it had turned up here at college!

Inside the envelope, there was something else — a note from Stefan written in an elegant hand. He'd picked the book up from the table they'd been sitting at, he wrote, when he had returned later to see if he'd left his Oyster travel card there — a loss, alas, he'd decided to put down to his unfortunate accident. She must have forgotten it in her rush to leave.

He could have returned it to the library, but the opening hours didn't coincide with his working day, so he'd returned it to the college reception instead. There, at the bottom of the page, was his mobile number and the words, *Thank you again for coming to my aid*.

For the rest of that day, when she wasn't trying to make sense of her lecture notes, thoughts of Stefan filled her head. Did she *want* to ring him? She reminded herself of her resolution to successfully complete the course so she could get a place at a decent university. There was no man in that equation. But perhaps she was getting ahead of herself. He'd told her how he wanted to become as familiar with the streets of London as he was with those of Vilnius. What harm would it do to suggest accompanying him on one of his walks next weekend?

That Friday evening, once the week's lectures were over, she dialled the number on the note.

Stefan had been delighted to hear from her and even more delighted by her suggestion. They arranged to meet up at Holborn Station the next day — Stefan had planned to make a tour of the Inns of Court, he said, but it would be much more interesting to have company.

It was a delightful walk. Helen knew very little of the history of London, apart from what she'd done at school, she told him, as they wandered past the parade of elegant chambers where fancy barristers plied their trade at exorbitant rates.

They'd been taken as a class to see the Tower of London, she said, but all she'd done was gawp at a boy she fancied all the way round.

'I wasn't very studious in those days,' she admitted.

Walking made conversation so much easier than sitting across a table in a restaurant where there was no way of avoiding making eye contact, and where she would have been beset with the uncomfortable feeling that what the two of them were doing must appear to anyone who saw them remarkably like being out on a date. When the last date you'd been on had been when you were 16, dates were scary. Walks, however, were just a nice, uncomplicated way of spending some time with a person you'd quite like to get to know better.

Their tour of the Inns of Court was the first walk they embarked on together. Over the next three weeks they met every Saturday, each time exploring a new area of London — or, in Helen's case, rediscovering it.

On Hampstead Heath, she told him about how long it had taken her to finally pluck up courage to enrol for the access course — two full years after she'd first picked up the prospectus from the library. It was after that walk that he'd brushed her cheek with an awkward kiss as they parted.

Walking alongside Camden Lock, she'd

talked a lot about her kids and how, if it hadn't been for them, she would never have had the confidence to enrol on a computer literacy course, which was the first step.

'I just wish I'd done it sooner,' she'd told him. 'But my ex-husband thought anything he didn't understand wasn't worth knowing about. He said I'd be wasting my time.'

'He sounds a charming man,' Stefan said.

It was on that walk that they held hands for the first time.

In Highgate Cemetery, in front of the statue of Karl Marx, she told him about Craig. About how they'd grown up and gone to school together. Then she'd got pregnant with Mandy and they'd got married. It was what people did where they came from, she said. But it had been a mistake from the first. He left when the children were in secondary school and she'd been on her own since.

Later, in the tea rooms at Waterlow Park, they'd shared a piece of carrot cake, laughing and brushing hands as they chased the last crumbs round the plate. She liked the fact that Stefan was shy and awkward, almost reverent in his behaviour towards her.

She was hardly the most sexually confident person on the planet. The only man she'd ever slept with was Craig. Perhaps Stefan sensed that the best way to proceed with her was to take things slowly. She wondered why he'd never married, but it didn't seem her place to ask just yet.

* * *

Helen sat in the canteen drinking a cup of weak tea from a plastic cup and worrying about her coursework. The last piece she'd got back had come with a disappointing mark and she was still smarting from her tutor's remarks about how, if she wanted to get a place at a decent university, she needed to put in more time and effort.

Glancing around at the shiny, young faces and hearing their enthusiastic babble, she felt a stab of something approaching envy. What she'd give for some of their energy! She found it so hard combining studying with the two cleaning jobs she'd been forced to take on to help fund her course and a social life. Only yesterday, she'd had to turn down an evening out with Stefan.

They'd fallen out about it, in fact. He'd rung her to tell her about a great Indian restaurant in Brixton he'd heard about. How did she fancy sampling the best curry in London tomorrow?

When she'd explained that she had a timed essay to do in class the next day on the biological importance of water, and so far hadn't even opened a book, she'd hoped for some sympathy. The reaction she'd got was anything but sympathetic.

Stefan had been loud and indignant. And when she'd tried to mollify him by suggesting they went at the weekend instead, he'd grown even more vociferous. It would be impossible to get a table at the weekend, he informed her, since this restaurant didn't take bookings. That's why he'd suggested going midweek.

She found herself apologising, even

though she couldn't possibly have known this. If she hadn't felt herself near to tears with exhaustion she wouldn't have said what she said next: 'I thought you understood how important this course was to me, Stefan'.

The change in Stefan had been dramatic. He immediately apologised. He'd acted selfishly, he said. Could she ever forgive him? The silly argument was over immediately.

This morning she'd received a text: *Am I back in your good books?* She'd texted back, *Of course you are x.* For a brief moment during their phone call, she'd felt uncomfortably like she was back in her marriage to a man with an unpredictable temper. But Stefan was nothing like Craig. He was kind, funny and a great companion. And he knew how to apologise, something Craig had never got the hang of.

She looked up to see Neil standing over her with a tray. Like everyone on the access course, herself included, Neil worked to fund his studies; he was a postman. Because he was up early, he needed to pack in more meals than most people. That had been his explanation when Helen once made a playful comment about how he always seemed to be eating, but never seemed to put on any weight.

'Looking forward to next Wednesday evening?' He sat down.

She nodded enthusiastically. Next Wednesday, there was to be a special seminar given by someone who worked as a forensic scientist. When it had been announced that it was compulsory, some of the younger students had groaned, but Helen, who'd always had a fascination for the subject since watching a gripping TV series, was really looking forward to it.

'It'll remind me why I enrolled on this course in the first place,' she said.

'I thought you wanted to do nursing.' Neil plunged his fork into the fattest chip on the plate.

'I do. But I like learning for the sake of it, too.'

He nodded affably. 'Right. I get you. Sometimes it's hard to remember that when it's one in the morning and you're lying awake worrying about your rubbish marks.'

Helen was surprised by this admission. Just this morning, in the ladies, she'd heard a couple of the girls on her course discussing how Neil was someone you could go to if you didn't understand something, and he'd always be able to explain it so that, by the end, you'd be convinced you'd come up with the explanation yourself.

'He's like your favourite uncle,' one of the girls had said. Helen had joined in their laughter, happy to be included. For the first time since she'd enrolled on the course, she felt like a student and not some ancient impostor.

She wondered about telling Neil what they'd said but decided against it. She sensed he'd be embarrassed by such praise. And then there was the other thing. If he thought he was in with a chance with any of those girls, he'd be gutted once he learned his nickname.

'Speaking of rubbish marks,' she said, getting up from her seat, 'I'm off now to work on the rewrite of my last feeble attempt at an essay.'

'Remember to read that chapter I told you about and you'll crack it,' Neil said.

'Thanks,' she said, as she moved away. 'Uncle Neil,' she almost added.

She worked solidly through the evening and was just about to drag herself to bed at nearly midnight when her phone rang. It was Stefan.

'I have some great news!'

'News?'

'My cousin has two free tickets to a concert at the Albert Hall on Wednesday night. Dvorak, Tchaikovsky and Ravel. And he gave them to me.'

'That's very generous of him.'

'No. Not really. He hates classical music. But you love it, I know.'

She'd told him so on one of their walks. A passing remark, but obviously he'd remembered.

'When did you say it was? Wednesday?'

She realised she was going to have to disappoint him again.

'Stefan, I can't come.' She explained about the compulsory seminar that fell on the same night. 'I'm really, really sorry.'

The silence on the line was heavy. It seemed to go on for ages. In awkward desperation, she struggled to fill it. Any other day and she'd have jumped at the chance, she said. She'd only ever seen the Albert Hall on TV. Just being inside, let alone listening to such lovely music, would have been a blissful experience! On and on she went.

'Then cancel. This opportunity at the Albert Hall will not come again.'

'Stefan. We've had this conversation before. I can't. My course is important to me.'

She fully expected another display of rage. Well, he could rage all he liked, she decided. This time she was ready for him. If he really couldn't understand how much her course meant to her, then it was probably best if they called it a day right here. But when he did eventually reply, his tone was polite, neutral.

'I'm sorry. I shouldn't have assumed you could drop everything just like that,' he said.

'We'll do it another time,' she assured him.

'No! There won't be a next time. Didn't you hear me? These tickets are a one-off!'

Helen recoiled at the barely-contained fury in his voice. Where had *that* sprung from? When he spoke again, he had it under control.

'But perhaps we can meet as usual next weekend?'

Helen couldn't help feeling unsettled by his unpredictable switch of mood.

'We'll see,' she said uneasily. 'Good night, Stefan. It's late and I've got an early start tomorrow.'

An hour later, she was woken by her phone ringing. It was a hysterical Stefan. Helen was awake immediately, her heart thumping with anger. Did he know what time it was? she asked.

'Never mind about the time,' he said, 'this is important. You have to listen to me. There's something you have to understand.'

2

Helen listened with increasing irritation to Stefan's rambling explanation. He wanted her to know he'd learned his lesson. He'd realised it was ridiculous to assume she could drop everything at a moment's notice, but he hoped that they could start again. With a day out, on Saturday.

'Are you mad? I have no intention of making plans for the weekend at this unearthly hour,' Helen spluttered. 'Go to bed, Stefan. Please.'

'OK, OK. I will. But only if you agree to see me on Saturday. If not a whole day, then how about half a day? Morning, afternoon, evening. It's up to you. I'm happy to fit in with you.'

'The only plans I've got right now are for going back to sleep. I've got a full day of college ahead, and afterwards I've got something else on.'

'What something else?'

The suspicion in his voice riled her.

'The job I told you about,' she snapped.

On two evenings a week she paid a visit to old Mrs Berry, who lived a couple of stops away on the bus. She'd done it for years, having answered an advert in the local newsagent's once while the kids were still at school.

A bit of light housework had been the initial job description. But, as Mrs Berry grew older and frailer, Helen had begun to take on more tasks. Because she liked Mrs Berry, she'd often stay on far longer than the hours she was paid for to chat, since the old lady thrived on company and had very little these days.

'Oh. Her,' said Stefan.

When she'd first mentioned helping Mrs Berry out, Stefan had seemed charmed. Here was yet another example of Helen's kindness, he'd insisted. Now, however, it was, 'Oh, her'.

'That's right,' she snapped. 'So, if you'll excuse me I'll say goodnight.'

Less than an hour later, she was woken again by her phone. What on earth could Stefan have to say that he hadn't said already?

'Helen. Please. Don't ignore me,' he pleaded.

'How can I ignore you if you keep calling me?'

'Just agree to see me and I won't call you again.'

Helen was in no mood for bargaining. 'I'm going to switch my phone off now, Stefan,' she said. 'If I were you, I'd get some sleep.'

Whatever Stefan said next, she didn't catch, as with one swift, decisive gesture, she cut the call. Sticking a pillow over her head she shut her eyes tight. Sleep, however, proved elusive, and it was as if she'd only been unconscious for ten minutes before her alarm went off.

Later, as she joined the noisy throng of students jostling to get to their classes, she felt like death warmed up. Being tired always put her in a bad mood. She was furious with everything and everybody — the bus for being late, the crowds of long-limbed students laughing and joking together and, most of all, Stefan for keeping her awake.

When she'd switched her phone on

earlier that morning, her inbox had been jammed with text messages from him. Further investigation had revealed half a dozen missed calls besides. Still angry with him, she'd deleted every one without opening them.

The first half of the morning dragged. Turning down Neil's offer of coffee together at break, she'd popped to the college shop for a bottle of water, planning to take it outside. It was cold, but the fresh air might wake her up.

Taking a detour through the common room, she grabbed the note she glimpsed sticking out of her pigeonhole. Could she go to reception, please, before the end of today, it said. What now, she wondered; couldn't people just leave her alone?

The receptionist seemed delighted to see her.

'My, my, aren't you the lucky girl!' she said. 'These are yours. From that posh shop by the station.'

She gestured to the impressive bouquet on the countertop, which was drawing admiring glances from the two other receptionists on either side of her. Helen, too, had noticed the flowers as she'd stood in line waiting to be attended to, but had assumed them to be some sort of floral display designed to make the college reception area look less bleak than it usually did.

'Those can't be for me, surely?' she said.

'If your name's Helen Walker, then yes, they certainly are,' the receptionist replied. 'They were delivered about an hour ago.'

'What am I supposed to do with them?' she asked. 'I can't exactly carry them about from room to room!'

The receptionist shot her an odd glance through her quivering lash extensions. Helen guessed she must sound churlish.

'Collect it at the end of the day, then. We'll leave it out here on display if you don't mind, and pretend it's for one of us. Don't you want to read the message?'

From the depths of the sumptuous blooms, the receptionist fished out a small card. Helen took it from her reluctantly. The message read: *Helen, you are not behaving like you should. Why won't you answer my calls? Stefan.*

Helen stared at the words for some

time, then crumpled the note in her fist.

'You know what,' she said, 'they look so nice on this counter. You keep them.'

Then she headed out for that fresh air she'd promised herself.

★ ★ ★

It was lunchtime. A troubled Helen hadn't been able to bring herself to return to class. She needed time to think about Stefan's bewildering behaviour and what to do about it.

She thought back to their first meeting, drinking tea together in the café. Should she have walked away like the others had when they saw he was all right after his accident? Was that when she'd made her first mistake?

'You know,' he'd said, when she'd complimented him on his English, 'I thought that if I practised, practised, practised then I would become so fluent that I couldn't fail to make many friends. But so far this has not happened. English people aren't very friendly, I think.'

And then she'd walked into his life.

Perfect timing. For him, but not for her. She'd wanted a friendship. Perhaps, in the longer run, something else, though that was an idea she'd never fully formulated. What she'd never wanted was this clinging dependence.

She decided to call him and tell him so. It was a relief when she was immediately transferred to answerphone and didn't have to talk to him direct. Her message was simple. She told him that it was probably best if they didn't see each other any more. He obviously wanted more of her than she was prepared to give. Her main priority was her work and she didn't think she could handle any distractions.

When she looked up, she saw Neil standing there.

'Where were you?' he said. He sat down and took a dog-eared file from the dilapidated canvas bag he carried. 'I took some notes if you want them.'

'Thanks, that was kind of you,' she murmured, taking them from him.

One of the many nice things about Neil was that he appeared to be totally devoid of curiosity. Since it was clear she had no intention of offering any explanations either for her absence or for her remarks on the phone just now, he didn't pursue it. Instead, he began to pore over the notes with her, occasionally apologising for his handwriting as she attempted to decipher his scrawl.

Half an hour passed quickly, during which time Helen didn't think about Stefan once. She managed to get through the afternoon without giving him too much thought, either. At break, she switched her phone back on, anxious that if he'd got her message he might have been trying to get back to her. But she had no missed calls and her message box was empty, apart from one from her tutor cancelling their half-term tutorial in a fortnight's time. Relieved, she switched it off again.

At the end of the day, as she scurried past reception to the main entrance, she averted her gaze from Stefan's bouquet, still in pride of place on the countertop. She was almost at the main exit when she heard footsteps behind her.

'Excuse me. Can I have a word?'

It was one of the receptionists. 'I hope you don't mind,' she said. 'It's about your flowers.'

'Oh, please. I was serious. Take them,' Helen said.

She was anxious to get away. But she could see that the youngest of the three receptionists who'd been on duty that morning — and the one who'd seemed the most sympathetic — was keen to say more.

'I just thought you should know. Because of what you did with the note and that. But there was a man in just after lunch, looking for you.'

Stefan had been here?

'Don't worry, he got nowhere. Not for want of trying. We didn't tell him where he could find you. It would be more than our jobs were worth to give out that sort of information.'

'I'm extremely grateful,' Helen said calmly, though inside she was in turmoil.

Nothing to thank her for, the receptionist said. They'd just been doing their jobs.

'How was he?' Helen asked. What she

meant was 'Did he seem crazy to you?'

'He was polite, friendly, quite flirty, actually,' the girl replied. 'Not with me so much, but with Jade, who flirts with everyone.' But even Jade wasn't so stupid as to give away information just because someone smiled at her. Jade, Helen guessed, was the one with the nails and the eyelash extensions.

'You know, if you're worried about him stalking you,' she said, 'perhaps you should report him to the police.'

Stalking? Had Helen heard her right?

'I'm sorry,' she said politely. 'I don't mean to be rude. But I've got a bus to catch.'

'Of course,' the receptionist said. 'I hope you don't think I was trying to frighten you . . . only if it were me, I'd want to know. That someone was looking for me, I mean.'

'Thanks,' she said. 'I appreciate your concern.'

On the bus all the way to Mrs Berry's, Helen kept thinking about what the girl had said. She'd seemed genuinely concerned that Stefan might be a danger to her. Could he have somehow given that impression with a look or a gesture?

Oh, but why should she take any notice of some 20-year-old kid? She was probably bored — who wouldn't be, doing her job? Making up scare stories was a way of passing the time. Stefan was harmless. Otherwise he'd surely have found some way of getting past Reception.

But all the same, she thought, hopping off the bus, she couldn't help feeling relieved that in all the time she'd known him she hadn't given him her address.

She threw herself into her chores. Cleaning always helped take her mind off things. Thankfully, Mrs Berry seemed quite content to stay put in her chair, listening to a concert on the radio, instead of following her from room to room as she sometimes did, distracting her.

She understood why the old lady seemed tired when she went into the kitchen, the last room she'd planned to clean. Laid out on a tray was Mrs B's best china teapot, alongside the matching milk jug, sugar bowl and two used cups and saucers. Two plates and the remains of a Battenberg cake explained the crumbs she'd just hoovered up from the living-room carpet.

'Been having visitors, Brenda?' she said on her return to the lounge, once she'd tidied everything away.

'Oh, goodness me!' Mrs Berry's hand flew to her face. Honestly, her memory these days was getting worse every day, she said. 'Did he find you?'

Helen stared at her blankly.

'Your friend. Foreign gentleman. Such a nice man. Now what was his name again?'

'Stefan?'

'Yes, that's it, dear.' Helen felt her knees begin to tremble. Groping for the nearest chair, she almost fell in it while Mrs Berry, oblivious to her distress, carried on with her story.

Had to let him in — poor man looked miserable. Wandering the streets for hours, he said, looking for your house. Just couldn't remember the address. So lucky he remembered you and I were friends and recalled my address: One Coronation Street. No one would forget that in a hurry, would they! We had such a laugh about it.

But she'd never told Stefan where Mrs Berry lived. Why would she? This could only mean one thing. He'd followed her here a few days ago. Wormed his way into the house of a vulnerable old woman. Gained her trust, even nipped across the road to buy a cake to share. Persuaded her to use her best tea things.

He'd known she'd be coming here after college — hadn't she said as much when he'd called her in the middle of the night? And he'd known she would find him out.

'Oh, dear. You're not going to tell my daughter any of this, are you? She's always telling me I'm a foolish old woman.'

The last thing she wanted was for Mrs Berry to think herself in any sort of danger. Because, actually, she wasn't. Stefan had shown the old lady the same delightful side of his nature that he'd presented Helen with that afternoon in the café the day she'd come to his aid, and in the tea rooms in the park when they'd shared a piece of cake. In fact, he'd probably made Mrs Berry's day.

Helen smiled. No, of course not, she

said. This was between themselves. Only she must promise her never, ever to let a stranger into her house again, whatever they might tell her. You could never be too sure.

'I won't,' said Mrs Berry with a rueful sigh. 'Though he was such a lovely man. He made me feel 30 years younger.'

Helen chose to ignore that remark. 'I must get on home,' she said, rising from her chair.

'Oh, I know. Places to go. People to see,' Mrs Berry jested. 'If you go right now, you'll just get the number 41. The one that drops you off on the corner of your street.'

Good. The last thing she wanted was a long and lonely wait at the bus stop and the 10-minute onward walk home in the dark that taking the number 11 would entail.

She was going to be sensible about things and not overreact, she told herself as, less than half an hour later, she let herself into the house. All this looking over her shoulder and quickening her pace each time she heard footsteps would lead to madness. But the first thing she did, even before she removed her coat, was to draw the curtains. Just in case Stefan, now in possession of her address, was loitering on her street, spying on her.

Helen spent an uneasy night. It was a relief when daytime came. Twice she got up to check the locks and to peep from behind her bedroom curtains to make sure there was no one watching the house. The last thing she did before she finally went to sleep was to turn off her phone. She had no intention of experiencing a repeat performance of the previous night.

As she closed her eyes, she remembered something she'd heard somewhere about how you could block callers you didn't want to hear from. It was quite an easy thing to do, apparently. Her last waking thought before sleep claimed her was that Neil would probably be able to tell her.

The rest of the week passed uneventfully. There were no calls from Stefan and no signs that anyone was spying on her. But to be on the safe side, she made sure her weekend was busy, spending Saturday afternoon in the library and accepting an invitation to the cinema with a few of the girls from her course, who seemed to have accepted her as one of their set, now they'd grown used to the fact that she was old enough to be their (very young) mother.

All day Sunday she caught up on chores, then spent the rest of the day immersed in her books. She didn't want to go out, she told herself, despite the blue sky she could see from the window of the room she'd set aside for a study. But at intervals throughout the day, a nagging voice kept whispering in her ear, insisting that Stefan was keeping her prisoner in her own home. He'll win in the end, it said, if you don't stand up to him.

★　★　★

Today was the day of the visiting forensics science officer who was giving the seminar. Helen was excited about it and, for the first time in a week, she felt relaxed. So it was a shock to find the postcard on her mat as she was leaving the house to go to college.

On the front was a picture of the main shopping street in Manchester. Curious, she turned it over. Written on the back were the words *Back soon*. No name, but Stefan's elegant handwriting was easy to recognise.

The image of the postcard hung over her all day like a threat. She struggled with even the simplest things and could barely concentrate. As for the seminar that she'd been so looking forward to — she sat through it in a daze. All she could think about was the fact that Stefan's absence had freed her only briefly and that, any day now, he'd be back. What fresh torments would he inflict on her then? she wondered.

'Want a lift?'

The seminar was over and people were beginning to drift away. Neil, with whom she'd barely exchanged a word all day, was waiting for her at the entrance. She accepted with alacrity; throughout the closing moments of the seminar, all she'd been able to think about was the fact that she was going to have to make her way home alone in the dark.

Neil chattered on about the seminar and how informative it had been all the way to her house, only pausing to take directions from her and otherwise seemingly content with the occasional noises of agreement she made when he gave his verdict on the topics the speaker had covered.

When he pulled up outside her house, he leaned across to open her side of the door.

'Are you all right?' he asked. 'Only, you've been a bit quiet for days now.'

Insisting that she was fine, she got out of the car and made her way down the path to her house. At the door, keys at the ready, she turned to wave at the car that was already disappearing down the street.

She wondered if perhaps she should have asked him to walk her to the door, so that she felt safer. But then she'd have had to tell him the whole sorry saga about how she'd got involved with someone she shouldn't have. She, a grown woman, a mother for God's sake, making such a schoolgirl error of judgment.

She'd been such a fool, encouraging Stefan the way she had. Always listen to your instincts was the one lesson in life she'd drummed into her children. Perhaps it was time for her to start listening to her own. She froze at the sound of rustling behind her. Out of the shadows stepped Stefan.

3

When Stefan stepped out of the dark right into her path, Helen suppressed a scream. Although instinct urged her to react, reason told her she mustn't.

Recently they'd had a lecture on the fight or flight response in mammals. If she could simply list the physiological changes that a frightened individual experienced, maybe she could stop the mounting fear in her own body.

One, blood is shunted from the digestive tract and directed into the muscles and limbs; two, the respiratory rate increases; three, sight sharpens and four, awareness intensifies. It helped. Already she felt calmer. Attempting to cover her fear with a light tone and a bright smile, she asked him what he was doing there.

'Didn't you get my postcard? I've been in Manchester on business,' he said. 'It's a great place. The people are so much warmer up there.'

'I got it today,' she said stiffly.

She really didn't want to enter into a discussion about warm northerners versus frosty southerners. But how was she going to get rid of him? The key to the house was a heavy weight in her hand. If she unlocked the door then Stefan was bound to assume he was invited in. Maybe if she showed herself unwilling to let him in, he'd simply force his way inside.

If you clenched your fist and held a key between forefinger and second finger, you could jab an assailant in the eye pretty successfully, so she'd heard. But perhaps she was getting ahead of herself. There was nothing threatening about Stefan's body language so far as she could see. On the contrary, he seemed relaxed and totally at ease. Although she hadn't done anything to upset him yet. Well, that was a state of affairs that was about to change. She opened her mouth to speak.

'What about my message? Didn't you get it?'

'Oh, that.' He waved it away as if saying she didn't want to see him again was of no consequence. 'You were upset. Angry.

Not surprising. I can be very stupid.'

'I meant it, Stefan. I need to focus on my course. This is not the right time for me to have a relationship with someone,' she said.

'For 'someone' substitute 'you',' she thought.

'Exactly, which is why I've come up with the best solution.'

She stared at him. Where was he going with this? She soon found out. His cousin had just informed him that the business needed a presence up in the north-west and Stefan was just the man.

Because it was a small family business just starting out, hiring staff at the moment would be too much of an expense, he went on. But if Helen gave up the course that was clearly causing her so much stress and moved up to Manchester, too, they could buy a nice house together and she could divide her time between doing it up and helping him get the new Manchester branch up and running.

Helen's mouth almost dropped open at Stefan's insouciance. Had he heard anything she'd said about how much she wanted to get a place at university? And where had he got the idea that she possessed any talent for interior design? Everything that had come out of his mouth was, quite simply, absurd.

'Stefan, I'm going to say this once more and I want you to listen very carefully,' she said. 'I am not about to give up my course and move to Manchester. Do you understand me?'

'You're tired,' he said, waving her words away. 'I expect you've had a long day. How was your seminar by the way? That was today, no?'

'It was good,' she said, almost in a whisper.

Why was she allowing this conversation to continue? she wondered. The answer presented itself immediately. For her own safety, it was important to keep on the right side of him.

'Who was that who dropped you off just now?' His brittle smile somehow failed to reach his eyes.

'Just a friend,' Helen said guardedly.

'Neil, was it?' he said, curling his lip.

'The postman?' That was Neil's part-time job.

Clearly Stefan remembered every single thing she told him. There was a long silence during which Stefan appeared deep in thought. Then suddenly he announced that his cousin was expecting him.

'You are tired, I can see.'

She nodded, too weak to speak. All she wanted was to be on the other side of that door, alone. When he said that he'd speak to her in the morning, she simply couldn't find the strength to repeat that he mustn't contact her again. She'd be banging her head against a brick wall. She understood that now.

The rest of the week passed her by in a daze. While all the others in her class spoke of nothing but their upcoming reviews with their tutors, Helen drifted from lesson to lesson simply going through the motions.

At least twice, she nearly confided in Neil that she was worried about what she'd got into with Stefan, but each time, just as she was about to open the conversation, it was interrupted by one of their classmates asking if it was OK to join them.

On Saturday, out shopping, she found herself walking past the same café where she'd taken Stefan for a cup of tea the day she'd come to his rescue after his accident. Exhausted from little sleep and from the constant checking behind her to make sure she wasn't being followed, she ducked inside. Unless she got hold of a reviving cup of strong coffee, she decided, she'd never make it home.

'Oh, hello.'

Helen returned the greeting, surprised by the girl behind the counter's familiarity.

'You were here a few Saturdays ago — with him. That man. I'm the Saturday girl, so nobody bothered me — if they had, I could have told them.'

'I'm sorry?' she said. 'I don't understand.'

All Helen wanted was a cup of coffee. It seemed it wasn't going to be that simple.

'You didn't leave it behind, you know.

Mandy — the woman you spoke to — my boss, said that someone had rung about a book they thought they'd left behind. She described you. Well, I was there. And you didn't. He took it.'

Helen stared at the girl uncomprehendingly.

'I saw what happened because I was clearing tables at the time. You went to the counter to pay and he leaned over, opened your bag, took out your phone, messed about with it, put it back, then leaned in and took your book. Then he put it in his own bag.'

Feeling suddenly light-headed, Helen put out her hand and grabbed the counter to steady herself. Meanwhile, the girl embellished her account with details. How she'd thought nothing of it at the time — assumed they were a couple, in which case, she supposed it was OK to put your hand into someone's bag and take something out, with permission, of course. But that didn't tally with someone ringing up to say she thought she'd left her book on the table.

'Because you hadn't, had you?'

'Did he come back? The man? To look

for something he thought he'd lost?'

Stefan had told her he'd found it when he came back to look for his Oyster card. The girl shook her head fervently.

'No.'

'Are you sure?'

She was positive. It was her job to clear the tables, she said, and if ever she found anything, it got put behind the counter in case whoever had lost it came back.

'I'm sorry,' Helen said. 'I have to go.'

'Are you all right? You've gone ever so white. How about a nice strong cup of tea?'

But Helen was already on her way out.

For the rest of the weekend, she stayed inside the house and watched trash TV. Although there was always college work to do, she just didn't have the energy for it. It was a relief when Monday arrived. Just the thought of being part of a crowd again soothed her.

She was on her way out when the post thudded through her door. A pile of buff envelopes all bearing the names of various estate agents lay on the mat. Bemused, she opened the first two. They both contained the details of property in various districts of Manchester. Stefan. It had to be.

'I'm not going to think about this now,' she said softly, scooping up the rest of the envelopes and shoving them, alongside the ones she'd opened, into her bag. Today was the day the bin men came. She'd drop them off in the nearest bin en route to the bus, she'd decided, unable to bear the thought of them still being in her house when she returned.

There was a message waiting for her that said she was to go and see her personal tutor at one o'clock. She couldn't imagine why Dr Watkins wanted to see her. Most of her dealings were with students who weren't up to the mark, and though Helen wasn't finding the course easy, she always attended lessons and handed her assignments in on time.

So the rap on the knuckles she got when she was admitted to Dr Watkins' office and told to take a seat came as a shock.

'You do know why you're here, Helen, I take it?' She peered at Helen from behind her rimless spectacles, her face flushed.

'I have no idea,' Helen said, which was the truth.

Dr Watkins shuffled the papers in front of her. She seemed slightly embarrassed by the task ahead. Finally, she found the paper she wanted. It was a list of dates, times and names. She pointed to last Friday's date. *10am*, it said. *Helen Walker*.

'Your review,' she said. 'You missed it. I waited 20 minutes for you, sent you several texts asking where you were and all of them were ignored. I find your lack of courtesy appalling, frankly, and not at all what I would have expected from a mature student.'

Helen stared at Dr Watkins open-mouthed. Admittedly, she'd had her phone switched off ever since her encounter with Stefan on her doorstep. But missing her review? That couldn't have been right.

'You cancelled it!' she blurted out.

'I can assure you I didn't.'

Helen scrabbled in her bag, frantically searching for her phone. She felt tears stinging her eyes. Once more, she was the naughty schoolgirl summoned to the head teacher's study for some major misdemeanour.

'But I have a text from you,' she said in her defence. 'Wait a minute and I'll find it.'

Dr Watkins sat back in her seat, assuming the body language of someone prepared to give an opponent the benefit of the doubt, but certain they had right on their side.

'I — I must have deleted it,' Helen stammered, scanning through her text messages and unable to find the one she wanted. 'But I can remember exactly what it said.'

An image of the Saturday girl in the café suddenly sprung up before her. Hadn't she said that Stefan had taken her phone from her bag and 'messed about with it'? What had he done? Got her important contact numbers? Who else's numbers had he stolen? And why? To cause mischief? To keep tabs on her? Why would anyone do anything so crazy?

'The thing is, Helen,' Dr Watkins said. 'These reviews are a way to monitor your progress. If you miss one, then you are at a distinct disadvantage. I have no time now until the end of term and by then, you may have lost your way so much that it will be impossible for you to catch up. You've already missed two deadlines for coursework.'

Had she? How was that possible? She had no idea. But, of course, deep down she knew exactly why. Stefan. Not just messing with her phone but messing with her head, too, so she forgot to listen or write things down that she needed to remember.

'I-I'm sorry,' she said. 'I've been having some bad stuff happening recently.'

'We all have bad stuff in our lives, Helen,' she said. 'The trick is not to let it affect our studies.'

Helen struggled so hard to hold herself together for the rest of the interview that by the time she was finally dismissed, she was limp with exhaustion. Her one idea, as, head down, she scooted down the narrow corridor towards the main exit, was to get right out of the building and run for cover.

When she saw Neil among the throng

heading her way, she prayed he wouldn't see her. No such luck. He was already approaching her, his eyes full of concern, asking what on earth was the matter and was there anything he could do. That was the moment she broke down and burst into tears.

Neil had decided strong drink was the answer, and since today was a half day there was no reason not to indulge in the large glass of red wine he set before her in the bar of The Dirty Duck, two streets away. Neil's local, by all accounts.

It took Helen a long time to explain everything that had happened so far with Stefan. It was a relief to get it all out. When her tale was finished, Helen felt spent. What she wanted more than anything was to lie down and go to sleep.

But that, Neil said, was not going to happen. He was taking her to the police station. Now. It was time to report Stefan for stalking. At first, she was reluctant. The police would judge her, she said. They'd say she'd been a fool to encourage him. Besides, what evidence did she have? She'd deleted his texts and phone messages. All she had were the house details that had arrived in the post, still stuffed at the bottom of her bag, because she'd forgotten to throw them away in the end. But they hadn't actually come from him.

Then her phone rang. She'd forgotten to turn it off again after her meeting with Dr Watkins when she'd checked her messages.

'It's him,' she said.

'Take it,' prompted Neil. 'Tell him your intentions.'

Reluctantly, she listened to what Stefan had to say. Had the house details arrived in the post yet? What did she think? Was she as excited as he was? It didn't seem to touch him that her replies were so evasive.

When Neil mouthed 'Tell him' at her, she screwed up her courage and did exactly that.

'You've ignored my wishes not to contact me, Stefan, so now I have to warn you that I'll be making a complaint against you to the police.'

There was a moment's silence before Stefan replied.

'But, Helen. You don't mean that. We're going to be married.'

She cut the call. 'Come on,' she said, turning to Neil. 'Let's do it. Now.'

★ ★ ★

It had been a long day. Neil had insisted on driving Helen back to her flat, stopping off to pick up pizza en route and apologising for his appetite, which, unlike Helen's where the reverse was true, increased at times of stress, he said.

'Look,' he said, as once inside her house and seated at the kitchen table, he tore the crust off his four seasons. 'It's not so bad. You made your statement. And she believed you. That detective.'

There was no denying that Neil was a born optimist. A sentiment Helen, picking at her Margherita, found difficult to share. Yes, the detective believed her all right. But she had so many reservations about the chances of getting Stefan to stop what he was doing that Helen had left the station far from reassured.

Their first encounter with the Met had

been at the front desk, where Helen, after a long wait to be seen, finally got to stammer out why she was there to the lugubrious-faced desk sergeant. It wasn't the most comfortable of situations, with people walking past and the phones going off every two minutes. Not to mention the desk sergeant looking her up and down suspiciously as if he didn't believe a word of any of it, before finally disappearing into the back office for ages.

Eventually, another officer — this time plain-clothed and female — emerged. Helen couldn't help being slightly more reassured that the officer dealing with her was a young woman. The crime of stalking was a reasonably new offence on the statute and most of the victims were female.

She was bound to be more sympathetic, she reasoned, given that police officers were only human. Perhaps the older officers still viewed stalking in the same way they'd once viewed domestic violence — as something between a couple and best kept out of.

All these thoughts and many more besides ran through Helen's mind as the detective introduced herself and asked Helen and Neil to accompany her to the interview room, where slowly and patiently, she teased out Helen's statement.

'So what happens now?' Neil had the presence of mind to ask, when they were through.

This was the bit that Helen — who by this time had totally given up on her pizza and passed it over to Neil who'd been eyeing it covetously now he'd demolished his own — still felt unhappy about so many hours later.

'You heard what she said, Neil. The only sure way to stop Stefan harassing me is to get a protection order.' She looked up from her empty plate, gloomily. 'And the only person who can get me one of those is a solicitor, who has to go to a judge. Solicitors cost money. And judges take their time.'

'But once they've found his address — and that won't take them any time — they'll pay him a visit. Who knows, they may even be round there now! They'll give him a stiff talking to and that'll be the end of it.'

'I hope you're right, Neil,' she said.

'Look, if you're worried, you can bring your stuff round to mine tonight. I haven't got a spare bed, but I've got a sofa. Which I'll sleep on, naturally.'

It was tempting. But what about tomorrow night? And all the other nights that followed? She couldn't spend the rest of her life hiding from Stefan.

'No, I'll be fine,' she said.

From the depths of her bag came the sound of her phone ringing. Helen held her breath.

'I'll answer it, if you'd rather not,' Neil said.

Meekly, Helen nodded her assent. Neil handed her her bag and with shaking hands she fished out her phone. The number was unknown.

'It's OK,' she said, relieved. 'It's not him. Maybe it's someone from the police.'

Hopefully ringing to tell her that they'd had strong words with Stefan and he was under no misapprehensions about what would happen to him if he tried to contact her again, either by phone or in person.

'Mrs Walker? It's Sergeant Wilkins. We spoke yesterday.' It was the lugubrious-faced one behind the desk.

'Have you arrested him? Did he admit that he's been stalking me?'

There was a beat before the officer replied.

'We picked him up, yes,' he said. 'But I'm afraid he had a very different story to tell.'

'What do you mean?'

'Put simply, he flatly denies your accusations. In fact, he claims that you've been stalking him. I'm going to have to ask you to come back to the station, Mrs Walker, to answer some questions.'

4

When Helen paid her second visit to the police station, she was led into a different interview room. This was much less welcoming than the previous one. In fact, it looked exactly the sort of room where a suspect would be grilled.

Yesterday, Detective Constable Kath Speed had appeared sympathetic. Now, she sat still and unsmiling, her eyes fixed on the picture postcards set out on the table.

'Recognise these, Helen?'

'That's one of the Temples at the Inns of Court,' she said. 'And that's the coat of arms of the Knights Templar, where the Inns of Court got their name from.'

'I don't think we need to have a history lesson, love,' the uniformed officer sitting next to DC Speed said.

'Well, what do you want, then?'

'Tell me about these postcards,' said DC Speed.

Helen cast her eyes over the display. Waterlow Park and Highgate Cemetery. St Paul's and Shakespeare's Globe. Brick Lane and Kew Gardens.

'Over a period of about three weeks, I visited some of the places on these cards with Stefan.'

'Only some?'

'Yes. I know Stefan wanted to visit Kew Gardens and do a tour of The Globe, but I stopped seeing him before those visits could happen.'

A look passed between her two interrogators. What was it? Helen wondered. Suspicion? Disbelief?

'Where did you get these postcards from?' she asked.

'Mr Timonin handed them over when we paid him a call,' DC Speed replied. 'He said you sent them. After he called time on your relationship. One a day, over a period of 12 days.'

'That's nonsense!'

At this, DC Speed turned every card over, one by one. Each one was addressed to Stefan in block capitals and each one bore her signature. Nothing else, just her name. Helen felt suddenly sick. She lunged forward and grabbed the nearest card.

'That's not my handwriting,' she said. 'And I never knew Stefan's address.' She felt helpless, like a character in some dystopian novel, who doesn't understand the rules.

'He's the one. Not me. He sent me all those details of houses up in Manchester. Or he gave my address away to estate agents, which amounts to the same thing. And where did he get my address from anyway?'

She could hear hysteria rising in her throat.

'I'm telling the truth,' she burst out frantically. 'You've got to believe me.'

'And I do, Mrs Walker. But I just have to make sure. We'll get an expert to compare your writing with this, but I know what I am expecting that to show.'

All the nervous energy that had been building up since she got the summons to the station earlier began to trickle away. Helen slumped in her chair.

'Stefan Timonin is a slippery customer.

It's not going to be easy to pin him down,' DC Speed said.

'Why can't you arrest him? How do you know he hasn't got form for doing this sort of thing back in his own country?'

They didn't know that, DC Speed said. They were trying to find out, but these things took time. It was a hard thing for Helen to have to understand, but she had to realise that, because they had no evidence, all they could do was keep an eye on him and warn her to be careful.

She reminded Helen how she'd deleted every text he'd ever sent her and every phone call, too. Based on nothing but her word against his, this would never come to trial. What was his crime, for one thing? Sending her flowers she didn't want? Turning up on her doorstep, to say he was back from his business trip? Helen sank back in her seat, once more feeling hopeless.

'But sooner or later he'll slip up and then we'll get him.' The detective collected up the postcards, then rose from her seat. 'Keep a diary. If he approaches you, write down the date and the time.

Any calls, keep them. Ditto messages.'

At the door, she handed Helen her card. 'If you feel you're in danger, any time, day or night, ring me,' she said.

Helen took it with a trembling hand and thanked her quietly. Outside in the sitting room, Neil was waiting, guarding the overnight bag he'd persuaded her to pack for a temporary stay in his flat. When she'd joked that they might not actually let her out, he'd reminded her that she was the victim here. Of course she would be free to go once she'd made mincemeat of Stefan's accusation. Helen had found his black-and-white view of the world strangely comforting.

Unfortunately, she couldn't say the same for his flat, which, though clean and tidy, seemed rather bleak and bare, with boxes stacked up one on top of the other in every room. Neil explained he hadn't been living there long. He'd moved in a few days before the college course had started and since then, he'd been so overwhelmed with work he just hadn't got round to making the place look more homely.

She couldn't complain about his culinary skills, however, which far surpassed her own.

'And now I'm going to put clean sheets on the bed for you,' he said, once they'd finished eating and she'd helped him clear away.

When Helen objected, saying she'd make do with the sofa, Neil insisted that he could sleep anywhere. Helen, on the other hand, needed a proper bed and a proper night's sleep.

She fell asleep to the sound of Neil pottering in the kitchen, putting things to rights while humming along to a piece of blues music she didn't recognise. She didn't wake up until next morning when he knocked on her door to inform her it was her turn for the bathroom.

Such a tiny living space meant that they spent the next hour dodging each other. Helen met Neil as she came out of the bathroom wearing his bathrobe, since she'd forgotten to pack her own, and there was an awkward little shuffle between them. But they managed to get past that and breakfast was quite a convivial affair. Then it was time to leave the house and get into the car, which was parked outside.

Neil was the first to see it. He slapped his forehead and swore, loudly and vociferously.

'What is it?' Helen followed his stunned gaze. All his tyres had been slashed.

'Stefan,' she said grimly. 'I'm going to phone Kath Speed.'

DC Speed was grateful for the call. But if Helen had imagined that she was about to jump in her car and head over to Stefan's house to arrest him, then sadly she was to be bitterly disappointed.

'Unless there are witnesses or CCTV cameras on your friend's street and they've clocked him doing the deed, I'm afraid there's nothing we can do about this apart from giving you a crime number so you can make a claim on the insurance,' she said.

'But it's him! I know it is!' Helen was close to tears. 'He's followed me here. Just as he followed me to the lady I clean for and just as he followed me home.'

'Please, try not to get upset, Helen. I'm

not unsympathetic, but you know it may not be him at all,' DC Speed said. 'I know that street. It's not in the most salubrious of areas. Anyone could have done it.'

'Oh, sure.' Helen was angry now. 'But not anybody did. Stefan did.'

'Helen, you really need to calm down.'

'Thanks for the advice. I'll try,' she snapped, cutting the call.

By now she was shaking with fury. Not to mention mortified that she'd involved Neil so deeply in all this. Not only did he have the bother of having to contact his insurance company, but he was also without wheels until he could afford to replace them. Plus she'd made him late for class.

'I'm so, so sorry to have got you involved in all this, Neil,' she said.

It was nothing, Neil insisted. That's what friends were for. She wasn't to worry about him. He could take care of himself and, if she'd let him, he could take care of her, too, since she was obviously far too distressed to take care of herself.

'I'll kill him,' she muttered. 'I know

where he lives now, thanks to DC Speed showing me those postcards. I'll go round there and tell him it's got to stop.'

'Here,' he said. 'You're not thinking straight. You need a hug.'

She felt his arms closing in around her, stilling her shaking limbs, calming her breath. Just for a moment, at least, she felt safe.

'Better now?' he said after a while.

She nodded.

'I have to go to college today, Neil,' she said, speaking her words into his chest, so they sounded muffled. 'I need to go and see Dr Watkins and explain why I've got so behind.'

'She'll understand,' he said, into her hair. 'I'll come with you if you like.'

'And I'll help you with your insurance claim, later,' she said. 'If you like.'

'I do.'

'We'd better get the bus, I suppose, then,' she added. 'If we're going to stand a cat's chance in hell of making it to the first period.'

But neither of them was in any great hurry to move just yet.

★ ★ ★

Don't go anywhere without me, Neil had said, when he left to go and pick his car up from the garage. That was half an hour ago. She'd reassured him she had no intention of moving away from her computer screen. Although Dr Watkins had been hugely understanding when she'd explained her situation, the work still had to be done.

But she was restless. There was only so long anybody could stay cooped up and Helen's limit was shorter than many. Besides, she missed her house — the bed, the shower, a decent mirror. She needed some fresh clothes, too.

Helen's tantrum on the phone to DC Speed had provoked a burst of activity in the detective. Once again, she'd sent someone round to have a word with Stefan, who, of course, had denied all knowledge of the incident.

But I think he's finally got the message, DC Speed had said this morning when she rang to enquire if Helen had anything new to report. Her words had left Helen feeling reassured. On the strength of them, she decided she'd be fine to pop back home. If she felt the least bit spooked, she'd leave immediately.

It was eerily quiet inside her house. Restlessly, she wandered from room to room, tidying as she went. She'd left in a hurry and hadn't had time to wash the two pottery mugs she'd put in the kitchen sink. But there was no sign of either anywhere. On further inspection, she saw that one had been washed and dried and put back in the cupboard and the second lay broken in several pieces in the kitchen bin.

Helen froze. Stefan had been here, she was absolutely convinced. There were other signs of tampering, too. Her favourite perfume had disappeared from her dressing table and when she opened her wardrobe door she had the feeling that some items had gone missing. The scarf she'd worn that chilly afternoon in Waterlow Park. The blue jumper she'd had on the day they'd first met and Stefan had revealed his unhappiness in living with a cousin he didn't get on with in a city where it was impossible to make friends.

The cousin. In a flash, Helen knew what she had to do. If the Lithuanian police weren't interested in finding out about Stefan, perhaps the cousin could help.

It took her 40 minutes to reach the street in south London where Stefan lived with his relative. He'd told her that the cousin worked from home, sending Stefan off each day to do the legwork. She prayed with all her heart that today was no exception because, frankly, her Plan B — which was to run like the clappers if Stefan answered — stank.

It was a shabby-looking house in a shabby-looking street. Helen rang the bell, already poised for flight as she heard the sound of footsteps approaching the door.

'Can I help you?' The man who opened the door shared Stefan's accent and his dark hair and eyebrows. He was surprisingly smartly dressed and fit-looking, too — not remotely like the couch potato Stefan had described.

'Are you Stefan's cousin?' she said.

'I am Andrius, yes,' he said. 'But

Stefan's not here.'

'That's good. I need to talk to you alone.'

'Please. Come in.' He seemed wary, as if he suspected that she might be bringing trouble to his door.

Forgoing the usual niceties, she cut straight to the chase.

'Tell me the truth,' she demanded. 'Stefan's been stalking me and I need to know if it's something he makes a habit of.'

Andrius went suddenly white. He muttered something under his breath in a language she didn't understand.

'Please,' he said. 'Sit.'

They'd moved through the narrow hallway, into a small room that at one time was probably a living room, but was now a makeshift office. Helen perched on the edge of the only chair in the room, anxious to hear what Andrius had to say. He told the story quickly and with little embellishment, as though it embarrassed him.

From his late teens, Stefan had started to become fixated with women, he explained — particularly those who were kind to him or who helped him when he was in trouble. A young teacher. A nurse . . .

'It makes sense.' Briefly Helen related the circumstances of her own first meeting with Stefan.

'He never harmed them,' Andrius went on. 'But, of course, it's very frightening for the victim. As I'm sure you know.'

She nodded.

'And dangerous for Stefan. Twice, three times he's been beaten up by relatives of girls he's stalked.'

Stefan's parents couldn't cope with the stress any more, Andrius went on. Stefan refused to see a psychiatrist, and didn't believe there was anything wrong with him.

'I said he should come to England and work with me. I promised to keep an eye on him. But I can't be with him all the time.' He made a pleading gesture with his hands. 'He's a grown man.'

'Yes, Andrius. Indeed I am.'

Neither of them had heard Stefan enter the house. He stood in the doorway, regarding both of them with glittering eyes. He was clearly agitated. It looked as if he was turning something over and over in his jacket pocket. Helen's heart began to beat furiously. Was it a knife? she wondered.

'What do you want with me, you two?' he demanded. 'You, my cousin. You're meant to be on my side. And you!'

He turned to Helen. From his pocket he drew out a broken shard of pottery. She recognised it immediately. It was a piece of the broken mug she'd found in her kitchen bin.

Don't agitate him, Andrius's swift glance in her direction seemed to say. But Helen didn't need to be told.

'I thought you liked me,' Stefan said. With his right hand he was holding the shard from the broken cup over his left wrist. 'But you're just like all the rest.'

'No, Stefan,' she said. 'That's not true. I can help you.'

'How?'

'How did you break my mug, Stefan?' she said. 'I expect it was an accident. A pity, it's my favourite. But never mind. If you give it back to me, I'm sure we can mend it.'

Helen felt a sudden stab of pity for Stefan and for everyone like him — so convinced that their way of seeing the world was the right one.

'We? You and me?'

'We'll get some help,' she said. 'Andrius knows someone he can call.' She glanced over at Stefan's cousin, who was slowly reaching for his phone.

'So, will you give that piece to me, Stefan?'

He shrugged. 'I guess. If you think the mug can be mended.'

'I do,' she said, holding out her hand for it. Stefan dropped it in her hand, whereupon she put it straight into her bag.

'I'd make the call in another room, if I were you,' Helen said, afraid that if Stefan heard the word ambulance, he might make a run for it.

It took 15 minutes for the ambulance to come. During that time, Stefan was quiet. He seemed to have forgotten all about her. Perhaps he'd moved on already to some other unsuspecting victim. Who knew what went on his head?

Some day, Helen thought, when the ambulance had left, she'd like to help people like him. Perhaps, instead of training to be a nurse who helped mend broken bodies, she could train to be a nurse who helped mend broken minds.

Stefan would get the treatment he needed, where he was going, the para-medic nurse had said. Helen and Andrius mustn't worry about him. Helen felt better about such reassurance, but she wondered about Andrius.

'You can visit him. Watch him improve,' she said, as he showed her to the door.

'You're very kind, Helen,' he said. 'I'm glad I met you.'

Helen smiled and waved a cheerful goodbye. But inside she didn't feel so cheerful. There was a long road ahead for Stefan and his family. All she could do was pray for them.

As she rounded the corner, she felt for her phone and dialled Neil's number. He answered immediately, sounding frantic.

'Where have you been?' he asked. 'I've been going crazy with worry.'

'I'm fine,' she said. 'Honest. Except . . .'

'What? What's the matter?'

'Do you think I could possibly have another one of your hugs?'

* * *

The atmosphere in the main hall was electric as parents, friends and families waited to applaud the entrance of the one person they'd come along to support. When it was Neil's turn to climb the steps to the stage and accept his certificate — a pass with Distinction — the whole place erupted.

Now it was Helen's turn. She'd always hated being the centre of attention but she managed to shake the Principal's hand and smile and say thank you without making too much of a fool of herself.

That was that, she thought. All over. But then the Special Guest — Minister for Something or Other — took it upon himself to have a word with her.

'So.' He clutched her hand in his sweaty paw. 'What next for you, Miss — er . . . ?'

'Walker,' she muttered. 'I'm going to university. To study nursing.'

'Your parents must be proud.' He smiled benignly.

Helen was flattered. He must think she looked very young. Either that or he'd spouted this line so many times tonight it had become second nature. She couldn't speak for her parents — but she could definitely speak for her children, both of whom were sitting in the audience applauding wildly.

'Unfortunately, both my parents are no longer with us,' she said.

'I'm sorry,' he said.

There was no need to be. They were in their holiday home in Marbella.

'But my boyfriend's jumping for joy,' she added, turning to wave at Neil who was giving her the thumbs up from the wings and grinning at her madly. 'And that'll do for me.'

THE END